D0291993

SHADOW ON THE LAND

SHADOW ON THE LAND

A WESTERN STORY

WAYNE D. OVERHOLSER

THORNDIKE PRESS
A part of Gale, Cengage Learning

GALE
CENGAGE Learning™

Detroit • New York • San Francisco • New Haven, Conn • Waterville, Maine • London

GALE
CENGAGE Learning

LIBRARY OF CONGRESS CATALOGING-IN-PUBLICATION DATA

Overholser, Wayne D., 1906–1996.
  Shadow on the land : a western story / by Wayne D. Overholser. —
    p. cm. — (Thorndike Press large print western)
    ISBN-13: 978-1-4104-2960-5
    ISBN-10: 1-4104-2960-1
    1. Large type books. I. Title. II. Series.
  PS3529.V33S53 2010
  813'.54—dc22   2010037048

Published in 2010 by arrangement with Golden West Literary Agency.

Printed in the United States of America
1 2 3 4 5 6 7 14 13 12 11 10

SHADOW ON THE LAND

CHAPTER ONE

The dark girl was not to be found. Lee Dawes had already taken two unsuccessful turns around the deck, and now he started again through the main cabin of the *Inland Belle,* which was pushing its way up the broad and winding Columbia gorge between Cascade Locks and The Dalles. The hot air of the interior washed around him as he entered the cabin, his features carefully masked against the curious stares.

He had made no effort to conceal his pursuit of the girl. A man had the right to seek what he wanted, and Lee Dawes knew what he wanted. Pausing near the bulkhead, he let his gaze run restlessly, disappointment a sharp blade in him.

He went on. At this hour on a river packet, languor reached its peak. Points of departure and destination were of no immediate importance. A good luncheon, such as only a luxury packet served, was nearly digested, the cabin was warm and pleasant, and the Columbia lay under a mild spring sun.

Men were predominant everywhere in the main cabin, their square-cut coats with short lapels, unbuttoned, high choker collars cutting into well-fed jowls or dissolving beneath beards. Most of them seemed unaware of Lee, but the few women in the group, elegant in their spring finery, made a quick, pleased appraisal of this man with the frown and the searching brown eyes.

"It's a shame," one of them was remarking. "The river's so romantic, and the railroads will spoil it all."

Lee found himself admitting that she had a point. He had expected to dislike river travel, as a good railroad man should, but it had not been so. He liked the ease and space, the good fellowship. The packet had the life that man has given mechanical things, unrushed and functioning perfectly. He could hear the pant of the steam engines below decks; he felt the beat of it in the soles of his feet through the high-piled carpeting and his well-shined boots. The only urgency was in a bell's loud *clanging*, signals to engine room and crew, which became insistent and quick in the rapids, while the *thump* of steam in the big chests grew fierce.

The need of motion was a prod in Lee

Dawes. Wheeling impatiently, he moved across to the archway of the bar. Someone was playing the piano — loudly and without skill — and a fat man in a checked suit was roused from his nap long enough to glare and curse angrily. Lee had remembered seeing him walk a small and unhappy dog on the Portland dock, rough and bitter with the task. Studying the bar, he saw the man's wife, a heavy woman wearing too much jewelry, and paying avid attention to the gray-bearded man with whom she was seated at one of the small tables.

"Honest to goodness, Frank," she was saying, "you get off the funniest things!"

Deborah was not here, and he could have admitted the fact with far less study. She would have stood out in this crowd as Mount Hood towered above the long, ragged skyline of the sweeping Cascades through which they were passing. He had not actually expected to find her, but he had hoped. And persistence was a strong characteristic of Lee Dawes.

Something close to anger began to rise in Lee. She was playing a deliberate game of hide-and-seek, leaving the seeking to him, and he was reaching the end of his patience. He had tried earlier to find her stateroom, but the purser had been more concerned about company rules than generous tips and a younger man's inner urgings. With a sense of failure, Lee turned out onto the starboard passage, stopping to lean thoughtfully against the railing.

The *Inland Belle* was pressing patiently on. It was just above the towns of Hood River and White Salmon, the last landings before The Dalles. The thought of reaching The Dalles without accomplishing his private purpose set up its worry in him. This interior country was broad and deep, and, if a man couldn't find a girl on a river packet, he would be more helpless there.

Lee faced the Oregon shore, a broken line where gigantic masses of earth and stone rose boldly against the softly brightened sky, clad thickly here in pine, there bare and tawny and studded with outcrops of basalt. He considered this gorge, with which he had become familiar in the North Bank fight, to be geometry gone mad. Ruled lines rose sheer, to break in pure right angles close under the heavens; again, sweeping curves sprang mightily above the water and bent upward. Nature, never thrifty, had given way to utter abandon when she fashioned this.

Lee drummed his fingers on the rail. He had to see Deborah Haig before he went for his final talk with John F. Stevens. He'd had

10

his first glimpse of her while the *Inland Belle* was loading in Portland. He and Stevens had come aboard separately, to travel as strangers, at Stevens's request. So, idling on deck and watching the figures coming up the gangplank, Lee had a good look at her in his first glance.

Deborah Haig was tall, but she wore the bit of extra height regally. Inner confidence was mirrored in the severely tailored suit that set off the long, clean lines of her body, the dark, exotic beauty of her face, which held a hint of fire even in repose. Something had happened inside Lee Dawes that was different from anything that had ever happened to him before. Her gaze had met his and passed on, but it had left a stirring memory in him, a warm and persistent pull that had remained.

He had seen her on deck after that, keeping always to herself. But at Cascade Locks he had cornered her on the fantail. She had been willing to talk — bright, relaxed, totally impersonal talk. She was going to The Dalles. She didn't know if she would remain there. There was this vagueness, but beneath it was something definite, something unspoken between them, and he was certain that she felt it, too.

Her voice was low, rather husky. Her eyes,

like his own, were dark brown. Her fine, black hair swept upward from a pert and heart-like face. Her red lips were full and sensitive, giving her words an inner meaning as she parried him expertly. There had been that moment, a too short moment, and he had got exactly nowhere.

The thing that brought him close to panic was the fact that The Dalles would be only a way point for him. Time was precious and fleeting, yet Deborah Haig was flinging these precious seconds away. He could not tell, even now, whether it was her plan to avoid or madden him.

Events were scheduled to break along the Deschutes River, like thunder crackling across a burned summer sky, and Lee was to have a main part on the firing line. But Deborah Haig would not know that. Now, Lee knew he had to make certain of this girl, for he felt that he would love her with as much fiery devotion as he would love this new battle for which those two giants, James J. Hill and Edward H. Harriman, were girding.

Lee crossed to port and lingered there, scanning the Washington shore. It had been the site of the Hill-Harriman fight — a fight that now, years later, still made robust talk in railroad circles. Here timbered slopes

12

rose from the river, while frequent bare slants seemed to fall from the sky, brown and rubble-strewn and dropping like a tilted wall into the Columbia.

Movement stirred Lee, and he glanced along the passage, only to look away in pretended indifference. A girl had stepped from the main cabin and was coming toward him, a slight girl, pretty and attractively dressed, but not the right one. Talking to her earlier, he had learned that she was Hanna Racine, from a ranch south of Madras, out to Portland on business and now going home.

She smiled as she passed him and went on along the passage to stand by the rail. Unlike most women he had known, he had an idea that she was totally unaware of the picture she made there, was no longer conscious of him. Wind played with her light brown hair and deepened the color of her cheeks, as her eyes somberly studied the muddy current against which the packet moved, the tiny whitecaps that ran swiftly and unpredictably, the bits of driftwood that bobbed by.

Suddenly she turned from the rail, her eyes searching the row of stateroom doors. Lee swung in the same instant. A shrill, penetrating sound, totally foreign to a river packet, had broken through his thoughts. Then he realized that it was the insistent whine of a dog. Puzzled, Lee moved forward, and the girl came his way, too.

"Is it the machinery?" she asked.

"No machine could get that much distress into a squeal." Lee looked again along the passage and saw it, a shaggy head and pair of forepaws that leaped into view behind a window, falling and leaping again to the accompaniment of urgent whines. He grinned. "There he is, and two guesses."

The girl looked worried. "One's enough. People who don't take care of dogs shouldn't have them."

It was the dog he had seen with the fat man in the checked suit. Willie, he remembered, was the dog's name. Without thinking, he tried the knob, and found that the door was unlocked. He looked hesitantly at Hanna. "Would this be breaking and entering?"

"Go ahead," she urged. "I'll hire a lawyer for you."

"It wouldn't do any good to go after them. Fatso's dreaming about prettier women than mamma, and mamma's having herself some dreams with a richer man than fatso."

Quickly Lee opened the door. Willie was out in two long bounds, a black, shaggy creature whose mongrel body surged with new-found affection. Lee stilled the ecstasy and, scratching the floppy ears, looked up at the girl. "The problem is still unsolved."

Her cheeks had colored, but she smiled. "If you'll go for a stroll, I think the pup will take care of the problem."

A leash was hanging over a chair near the door, and Lee snatched it up, hastily pulling the door shut. He snapped the strap onto Willie's collar. "Two turns, Willie. Wait here, Miss Racine. I may need a witness before I get him back."

"I'll swear to the necessity."

Two turns around the deck, and Lee knew that Willie was not going to do the rest. Thinking that privacy was a requisite, he took the dog to the freight deck. Willie prospected. He whimpered. He trembled. But his training days were still fresh in his memory. The cuffs had taught him that wooden floors are inviolable. And the *Inland Belle* afforded nothing but unending wooden deck.

With the leash wrapping around his legs, Lee searched his brain. He scratched the woolly ears again. "For five bucks maybe we could get the pilot to stop at the next island."

They went disconsolately up the companionway to the passenger deck. Hanna turned inquiringly from the rail, but Lee shook his head. "Willie's baffled. All floors."

She frowned thoughtfully. "Willie, you show poor taste in your choice of owners."

"But good taste when it comes to picking friends."

She met his eyes, smiling. "That's right, and we can't let him down. What's in the main cabin that might attract him?"

"Why, nothing. . . ." Then a quick grin broke across his lean face. "Artificial palm trees." He shook his head. "No good. The purser would come charging out of his office with a horse pistol."

"I can handle him." Assurance gleamed in Hanna's eyes. "Give me three minutes."

It took three minutes for Lee to screw up his courage. He made a turn around the fantail and came back to the Oregon side of the boat. With Willie on short leash and his overcoat spread, Lee turned quickly into the main cabin. Briefly he noted that Hanna was at the purser's wicket across the way, and there was little doubt that at the moment the boat officer was wishing himself twenty years younger. Willie made no sound, and no eyes turned curiously to Lee. Nor was anyone at the piano. They cut from sight. When they emerged again, turning

16

quickly into the deck, man and dog walked easier.

They met Hanna before the door of the stateroom that was Willie's prison. Lee opened the door and pushed the dog in, closing his ears to the protesting whimpers.

"That was a nice thing to do, Mister Dawes."

A warm feeling washed through Lee. For a moment he almost wished there was no dark-eyed distraction aboard the packet. This was a nice girl, a warm and sympathetic girl — and a pretty one.

They stood together for a time, eyes on the Washington hills, feeling the mutual bond that comes to people when they have done a good job together. Lee's mind turned back over the past few years, and for the moment he forgot Hanna and the dog. To him the Columbia Gorge represented a battleground, reminding him of the days when he had fought down it as a special agent for James Jerome Hill, mentor of the Great Northern. It was a reminder of a triumph, for it was a fight they had won as decisively as they would win the struggle now shaping.

The Columbia had no duplicate. Originating in the wilds of Canada, it twisted down through the bare, brown flats of Eastern

Washington, turning westward through Wallula Gap, carving a deep course through the basalt here in the gorge, and rolling on in massive power to the Pacific. It was wild terrain, over which many had puzzled and fought, from the time the Indians had first told stories of a great river in the West, stories that drifted across the continent to restless men ever dreaming of an empire — and a channel of empire it had become.

He saw it again in a swift flow of pageantry. Lewis and Clark. The mountain men, buckskinned and bearded, fortitude and long rifles their weapons, beaver plews and adventure their prize. Hudson's Bay Company and the *voyageurs,* beribboned and singing, as their paddles cut the river. Missionaries preaching of peace, and unwittingly bringing a racial war. Ox trains plodding to the vast Oregon country, driven by stout men who cried for elbow room. The 'Forty-Niners crossing a continent in their lust for gold. These were the beats of empire that the river had known and pondered without change as it rolled westward!

Then the steel bands, and the empire was endowed with speed. No longer would land-seekers pile up east of the Big Muddy, or raise dust plumes on the plains, or leave in that vast emptiness the whitened bones and steel and hickory skeletons of wrecked Conestogas.

The wheel ruts dimmed. Steel glistened with use. Bright, this land to the westward, and giants were reaching to claim it. Struggle had come here in the gorge, and it was coming again along the Deschutes. The North Bank fight had been bitter and ruthless. For reasons clear only to the industrial giants of Wall Street, the thriving city of Portland had been slow to come under serious consideration as a major Western rail terminal. Only belatedly had it been linked with San Francisco by a coastwise section of the Southern Pacific. Henry Villard had built a line westward through the Columbia Gorge, and later the Union Pacific had extended its system from Ogden to Baker, and the long-sought link was fitted into place. Thus, by 1909, Portland and the state of Oregon were dominated by the Harriman enterprises.

It was at a Lewis and Clark Exposition banquet in Portland, in 1905, that James J. Hill had first declared his intention of entering and developing the state that had so long remained largely an island of transportation enclosed by rails. Hill's first move was to propose a branch line of his Great Northern, swinging down from Spokane and reaching Portland by the north bank of the Columbia. Harriman rose to beat off the challenger. Mile by mile, foot by foot, these giants of the twin rails had fought for possession of the North Bank. The federal courts became a battleground. They carried the fight into the gorge and at times into the water, laborers resorting to pick handles, crowbars, and lusty profanity as the conflict was fought out to its bitter end. Hill had triumphed and built his line, and now the rivalry between the two was keen and constant.

Lee felt a stab of pain as he remembered the personal cost of this fight. Somewhere in that sound and fury his warmest friend had become a bitter enemy. Mike Quinn was a better man to fight beside than against, a man to travel with, yet a man whose brittle temper and instinctive rivalry, so far as Lee Dawes was concerned, had made that impossible.

Wondering where Quinn was now, Lee visualized the rugged face, thought briefly about their years together. He had not heard of Quinn for nearly two years, and he thought grimly that this battle about to break out along a hundred-mile stretch of cañon would seem strange without Quinn on one side or the other.

"It's beautiful here," Hanna said, her voice breaking into Lee's abstraction. "Man destroys a lot of things, but he will never destroy this."

"It's strange that this country was overlooked so long," Lee murmured.

"People have different ideas about that. Some of us think we're living in a world that has grown old and crowded, and are glad that it still has a few places like this for the hungry to go to. Others think there is nothing here except another field for them to exploit."

He stared at the seriousness that was in her. There was a personal inflection to her words, a bitterness that he did not understand. He said: "Sounds like you had a grudge against somebody."

She shook her head. "No. Let's call it a matter of principle. I want this country to belong to the people."

Lee had never heard a woman talk that way before. To him a woman was to be pursued, to be caught and kissed and forgotten when the loving was done. Life was a matter of greeting a new day, a new fight, a new woman. It was an exciting and eternal game, was this business of Lee Dawes's living. And here beside him was a woman well graced for his kind of life, yet

21

talking in terms that both interested and puzzled him.

"There is no peace here in the Northwest," Hanna went on. "In Crook County, where I live, sheepmen and cattlemen still fight, and settlers try to make a living on new irrigation projects, while they keep their hopes for a railroad." She shook her head. "It's a land bright with promise, but it has the shadow of selfish men across it."

"Maybe we should cut those men down to size," Lee said lightly. "Then their shadow wouldn't be so long."

Lee stood smiling at her, thinking how different this girl's attitude was from anyone else's he had heard talk, and so utterly different from his own. He had never ducked a fight, and had at times gone out of his way to find one. He drew a deep breath into his great lungs. Six feet one, one hundred and eighty pounds of hard bone and muscle, Lee Dawes was built for conflict, to seek it, to thrive upon it. He was lithe and rugged and swift moving, and yet this slim, assured girl frightened him a little.

"It's not so easy to cut them down," Hanna said.

Lee was aware that she was irritated by the lightness of his manner, and he was aware, too, that the *Inland Belle* had kept

22

traveling, that his personal problem was as big as ever. Examining his watch, he said: "It has been a pleasure, Miss Racine." He lifted his derby, and smiled. "I hope we meet again." Nodding, he replaced his hat, and walked swiftly away.

Lee turned forward and rounded the deckhouse, coming back on the port side. Then abruptly he was hurrying his steps, for Deborah Haig had come out of a stateroom down deck, had glanced at him impersonally, and turned away. Lee came up to her, and succeeded in maneuvering her against the rail.

"I've been looking for you," he said.

"I have to see the purser, Mister Dawes."

"He'll wait. It's more important that you tell me where you live and where I can find you."

"Why is that important?"

Her smile was quick and tantalizing, her dark eyes reflective, and Lee felt that she was measuring him. He had a naked sense, then, as if she had gained an insight into the secret places of his mind. He said a little roughly: "You know what we could mean to each other."

"I wouldn't give you the satisfaction of. . . ."

The steward who had come from the main

cabin paused. "Mister Dawes," he said.

Lee frowned, knowing that opportunity had slipped away again, and that he still had gained nothing. "Yes?"

"The gentleman in S-Eight wants to see you at once, sir. He said to make it clear that he means right now."

Lee nodded, but before the steward had left, Deborah Haig had slipped away, her lips holding a soft, triumphant smile. Lee turned down the deck, and then it was that he saw Hanna Racine. She had crossed to this side of the boat, and had watched, smiling in dry amusement.

CHAPTER TWO

The gentleman in S-8 was an average-sized man, perhaps sixty, his mustache more gray than black, and the rugged quality of his face did not conceal a sense of force and quick, keen intelligence. It was a practical intelligence, but there was also a sensitiveness about him, of one whose vision ranges beyond habitual horizons. He was a man who could not only plan but accomplish — abilities that had prompted James J. Hill to call him the greatest location engineer in the world.

John F. Stevens had helped Jim Hill throw the steel bands of the Great Northern across the vast Northwest to Puget Sound. His discovery of Marias Pass, north of Butte, had lopped off seventy miles of the distance traveled by the rival Northern Pacific. And he had been chief engineer of the Panama Canal.

Stevens waved Lee to a chair, and studied

him thoughtfully. Lee, looking at Stevens, felt the excitement that was in the engineer. Again the warning suspicion rose in Lee's mind that the new enterprise was far bigger than he had been led to believe.

"I'm afraid I was delayed by the beauties of the gorge," Lee said guiltily.

"The one I noticed you with was a real beauty. I saw you helping her walk a dog." Stevens jerked a thumb toward the slatted cabin window through which the outer light painted bars of gold and black shadow across the deck and up onto the bunk. "When I was watching you, Dawes, I wished I was thirty years younger and as handsome." He paused, and added with thin irony: "But, in case you've forgotten, we're here to build a railroad."

Lee shifted uncomfortably and waited. His one previous talk with Stevens had gone only into the matter of Lee's availability and his acceptance of this job. Now the details would come.

"The North Bank was no Sunday school picnic," Stevens went on, "but this one will be tougher. Absolute secrecy is essential at the moment. You're working for the Oregon Trunk. Beyond that you know nothing."

Lee grinned. "I savvy, but there's plenty of talk about Hill backing the Oregon

Trunk."

"There'd have been more if we'd come by train. We stole a march on the Harriman sleuths by coming this way. The point is we jumped the gun too soon on the North Bank. Let folks know ahead of time you want a right of way, and you have tripled the cost." Stevens shrugged. "However, the cost of our right of way is the smallest of our problems. Right now I'd like to keep the Harriman people guessing. At the moment we admit we're building to Madras, but the folks on south will continue to hope."

Stevens smiled. "The stakes are high. For that reason, I won't know you, or you me, after you leave this cabin. You'll go to Shaniko by way of Harriman's Columbia Southern. Take the southbound stage to Madras. Stay there a few days, and then go on to Bend." Stevens leaned forward. "You don't need to make a secret of the fact that you're working for the Oregon Trunk. Encourage others to talk. Your part is to listen. Probably you'll have some Harriman sleuths on your trail. I've had some on mine."

"Sounds like fun." Lee's face was that of a small boy reaching ahead in his mind to a circus coming to town. "I like to fight."

"We'll have one, Dawes, but this business of your liking a fight is both a weakness and a strength in you. See that your fighting is limited to matters concerning the Oregon Trunk. A dead man won't help us."

"It can't be that serious."

"It can be exactly that." Stevens began pacing the floor. "Some things have happened that don't look like Harriman's tricks. Let's say there's a clouded element somewhere, perhaps a third party who wants us and the Harriman people to cut each other's throats."

Lee canted his chair back against the wall, long legs bent, heels hooking a chair rung. "A three-cornered fight," he murmured.

"It looks that way." Stevens drew a map of Oregon from his pocket, and spread it out on the berth. "Before we talk about that, I want you to get a picture of the battle-ground in your mind."

Lee rose and watched over Stevens's shoulder while the engineer ran his finger along the Deschutes River, from its head in the high Cascades to where it emptied into the Columbia a dozen miles from The Dalles.

"The Deschutes drains a number of lakes and runs an even stream all year. The Metolius River and the Crooked River come in here. From there on down, the Deschutes twists through one of the most fantastic cañons in the world." Stevens slid his finger upstream to Bend. "Here the altitude is thirty-six hundred feet. It's nearly sea level where it comes into the Columbia. Now you can see why this cañon is the one good entry into central Oregon. Our control of this water grade is vital, and the outfit that controls it will be the one that establishes the principle of 'first construction and use' at the narrow places where there is room for only one railroad."

"So we'll have railroad exploding all over the cañon." Lee shook his head. "Doesn't seem to be much sense in having a ruckus like this over a patch of sagebrush, if that's all this is."

Stevens glanced at him sharply. "You have the same mistaken idea a lot of people have, Dawes. Even if we go no farther than Bend, the resources in central Oregon are so staggering that a railroad would be worthwhile. It's a cattle and sheep range. The desert east of Bend may become a wheat country. A number of irrigation projects are being developed around Bend. And" — Stevens tapped his finger on the map where the slope of the Cascades broke eastward toward the desert — "there is the largest stand of virgin pine in the United States."

Lee showed his surprise. "Sounds like a treasure chest."

"That's what it is." Stevens folded the map and slipped it into his pocket. "Now about your job. You have two major assignments. First, find out who this third party is, and do what needs to be done to checkmate him. Meanwhile, you'll be a sort of general chore boy to cover your real business. You'll buy some right of way between Madras and Bend, so that people will know who you are. It's possible that as soon as your identity is established, our third party will make himself known. I have an idea what it is, but not who. If you've followed the papers, you've read of the state-owned railroad movement."

"That's a hell of an idea," Lee said.

Stevens nodded. "It is from a railroad man's standpoint. The thing that started it is the fact that large areas of Oregon, such as this Deschutes country, have no railroads. Harriman has made promises, and a dozen rumors have flooded the country. Harriman has even talked about extending his Columbia Southern south from Shaniko. Well" — Stevens spread his hands — "the people in the interior have seen no steel being laid.

All the rumors have turned out to be hot air."

"Harriman never did anything on the North Bank until Jim Hill moved in," Lee said.

"And it's Hill who's starting him up the Deschutes." Stevens tapped the map thoughtfully against a knee. "Not long ago I made a fishing trip into the Bend country and on down the Deschutes. I landed some rainbows." He smiled. "I told one man I was going to start a fish hatchery at the mouth of Trout Creek. What's more to the point is that I got a right of way. It's a real trip down that river, Dawes . . . wild water, two thousand foot cliffs, rattlesnakes, and some stubborn ranchers who don't think much of a railroad. The Oregon Trunk has a survey up the cañon, but it has done very little besides that. The controlling interest belonged to Billy Nelson, and I bought him out."

"For Hill?"

Stevens's eyes twinkled. "Keep guessing, Dawes. It's just as well you don't know everything right now. When the Oregon Trunk got serious about a railroad, it ran into trouble with the Bureau of Reclamation, which had an idea about building a power dam on the Deschutes. So we were hung up, and central Oregon still didn't have a railroad."

"Then that's what is behind the state-owned railroad?"

Stevens nodded. "That's part of it. We got the trouble with the Bureau of Reclamation straightened out, but the state-owned railroad proposal will be on the ballot at the next general election. Now Harriman has promised the governor they'll get started, but he's abandoned the Columbia Southern. The grade to the top of the plateau is too tough. They've formed the Deschutes Railroad Company, which will come up the cañon. When Porter Brothers moved a couple of barge loads of grading machinery for us across the Columbia to the mouth of the Deschutes, it was like setting off a charge of dynamite under Ed Harriman's chair."

Lee laughed. "It'll be a case of who gets there fastest with the mostest railroad."

"That's it. Don't underestimate the importance of getting our missing pieces of right of way. What we've got now is like a checkerboard. Some of the leases and entry rights the Oregon Trunk had have lapsed, and we've got to beat Harriman to them."

Lee's grin was quick and confident. "I'll beat them."

Stevens raised a hand. "Don't be too sure. That brings me to your second assignment. There's one piece of property between Madras and Crooked River that's going to be hard to get a right of way through, and it's vital. Crooked River gorge is about four hundred feet deep, but there's one narrow place where we can bridge it. This property I mentioned belongs to a girl named Hanna Racine, and it's strategic because it controls the approach to this crossing." Stevens paused, eyes on Lee. "What's the matter?"

"Did you say Hanna Racine?" Lee asked weakly.

"Yes. Do you know the girl?"

"I've heard the name," Lee admitted, thinking of how he had abruptly left her at the rail when he'd gone looking for Deborah Haig.

"Her father was a big rancher and a very well known man in Crook County," Stevens went on. "And I'll say that Herb Racine was just about the toughest old codger I ever ran into. Hated both Hill and Harriman. He did a lot of work getting this people's railroad movement started. When he was killed about a year ago, his daughter inherited the ranch, and I'm sorry to say she inherited his prejudices and economic theories." Stevens smiled. "That's the story, son. You have a reputation for making women like you, so I don't think you'll fail."

Lee rose and reached for his hat, thinking sourly that he hadn't lived up to his reputation with Hanna Racine. "Do I have a free hand?" he asked.

"The sky's the limit." Stevens glanced through the window. "We seem to be getting in." Rising, he handed Lee a checkbook, a power of attorney, and a handful of forms. "Any of our agents could buy most of the missing pieces, but the Racine property will take all of your special talents."

"I'll try to make use of those talents."

Stevens offered his hand. "Good luck, Dawes. I want regular reports. Send them to the OTL in Portland. Within a week or so, go on to Bend and stay at the Pilot Butte Inn. I'll send you detailed instructions there. Later, you'll be working with Porter Brothers, who are doing our construction for us. They'll put in a camp at Horseshoe Bend, which is in the lower cañon and a trouble spot. Another camp will go in at Charley U'Rens's place above White Horse rapids. One of our main problems is getting materials into the cañon. Some will go out over the Great Southern to Dufur on the west side and then be freighted down to the Deschutes, but the bulk of it will go over Harri-

34

man's Columbia Southern on the east side and be ferried across the river. Later, you'll be working on some of those access problems. They'll be tough nuts to crack." He shook his head, and then, eyes twinkling, he added: "And don't get too distracted by the beauties you'll find along the Deschutes."

"I'll remember that, sir," Lee said, sobered by the magnitude of this race, and by the error he had already unwittingly made. Lee stepped out of the stateroom, thinking again of a certain skirt that flicked so fetchingly above a certain pair of pretty ankles, and, as he turned along the deck, he noted that they were rounding Crates Point, which meant they would soon be in.

Then he saw Deborah Haig. She disappeared from sight forward, and he followed in long, quick strides. She vanished into her cabin as he rounded the bow, hurrying as if she realized he was following. Lee found the door shut when he reached her cabin. Without knocking, he turned the knob and stepped in, closing the door behind him.

The girl whirled, anger sparking brightly in her eyes. "What right . . . ?"

"You ran, but you knew I'd follow, so you didn't lock the door. Wasn't it Eve who started this game with Adam?"

"I thought you were a gentleman."

"Gentleman?" Lee laughed. "Not any. We'll be landing in ten minutes. Let me take you to supper tonight."

Deborah looked at him thoughtfully, with the cool judgment of an experienced and mature woman. "You have a way with you, Dawes."

"What's that got to do with supper?"

"I was thinking of another time. The answer is no. I'm meeting somebody."

"A man?"

"Perhaps."

"Deborah, we've got to meet again. We couldn't be thrown together like this and do nothing about it. Lady Luck wouldn't give us another chance." He came closer, eyes utterly serious. "If I've offended you, I'm sorry."

"A persuasive speech, Mister Dawes. I'll make you a trade. Tell me where you're heading, and I'll tell you if we'll meet again."

He was instantly on the defensive, feeling the prying quality of her offer. The girl sensed his thought, and the friendliness abruptly left her eyes. There was a short moment of inner debate in him. Then he said, against his better judgment: "Shaniko."

Deborah's smile came quickly. "Why, so am I."

"Supper there?"

"Why not just wait and ask me there." There was more promise in her eyes than he had expected. "Will your friend be with you?"

His eyes narrowed. "What friend?"

"Oh, the steward said some man wanted to see you."

"It wasn't important. Not like seeing you in Shaniko."

He drew her into his arms, and, when there was no resistance, fire crept into his lips as he pressed them against hers. She was limp and clinging, and a flame touched them, and he sensed that she, too, felt it. Then she pulled from him as abruptly as she had submitted.

"It was easy, wasn't it, Dawes? I wonder if you have ever kissed a woman seriously."

"What did you think that was?"

"A trial, I'd say." Her breath made a little sigh. "I guess you'd better go. We're landing."

Lee paused at the door, his eyes on her speculatively. "Shaniko," he said, and left the cabin.

He found himself directly in the path of Hanna Racine. She went past him, her eyes showing no sign of recognition. Lee, turning toward his own cabin for his luggage, felt a sudden uneasiness grip him. He had no way of determining whether Hanna knew whose cabin he had been leaving, but, judging by the way she had hurried by, he was afraid she did. A fine start he had made in this gigantic chess game John Stevens was playing.

The *Inland Belle* was cutting in slowly to the landing, the big stern wheel seeming to walk across the water. Lee stood at the rail on the shore side, his grips at his feet. The Dalles spread before his eyes on a flat beneath the huge, brown hills. This was the entrance to much of central Oregon — a romantic town that had seen settlers pouring in from the East and miners heading eastward to the gold-bearing streams. He had been here during the North Bank fight, crossing on the ferryboat from Grand Dalles, where the Hill line had its station. But there was little here now to attract him. One word kept ringing in his ears: "Shaniko!"

Hanna Racine hurried past, and waited with a studied soberness for the gangplank to be run out. The passengers crowded by, and with some amusement he saw the fat owner of the dog, Willie, come down the passage. His wife was with him, but it was the man who was having the trouble. His arms were piled with luggage that teetered uncertainly, and somewhere in that tangle of arms and hands and bags he found a finger to grip Willie's leash.

"Get a move on," his wife was saying ominously.

It was then Willie saw Lee, and he promptly raced across the passage, pulling his leash across the fat man's legs. The man stumbled, and a valise bounced to the deck. Willie, disconcerted at finding himself unable to reach the tall man who had become the object of his affections, lunged again, and the fat one, legs tangled, went crashing down in a scattering of luggage. He swore and came to his knees, eyes blazing. He cuffed the dog savagely, and cursed again.

"Don't do that!" Lee bent threateningly. "Dog beaters come right down at the bottom of the pile."

"You saw him trip me."

"Don't you want him?"

"Want him? Hell, I'd like to drown him."

Lee dangled a $10 bill in front of him. "I want him."

"Horace, don't let him have Willie!" the woman screamed.

The fat man grinned at her as he reached for the money. "Maybe I should take up the matter of you drinking gin slings all day with Pete Royce. I'm tired of walking this dog. I'm tired of dog biscuits on the floor. I'm tired of having dog hair on my pants. You say he's yours, but I'm the dog maid."

The woman sighed, and turned away. The fat man stuffed the money into his pocket, gathered up his luggage, and hurried after his wife. Lee, Willie's leash in his hand, watched them go. Hanna Racine had disappeared. Still Lee waited, seeing a way to regain lost ground with Hanna, and wanting to talk to Deborah again before she went ashore.

Then Lee's eyes fixed on a man standing on the wharf boat, his gaze pinned on the gangplank. A big man, only a little shorter than Lee and even wider of shoulder. The craggy Irish face, the sandy hair, the sprinkling of freckles — all familiar to Lee Dawes. So, too, were the big hands familiar, knuckles that Lee had felt on more than one occasion. Lee drew back slightly, knowing that Mike Quinn had not seen him and not wanting him to. And he thought swiftly of what this meant.

Lee, his attention on Quinn, did not see Deborah until she had hurried past. She turned down the gangplank, her body tall and perfectly molded. Then Quinn left his station, elbowing eagerly through the crowd.

They met at the foot of the gangplank, and the girl went into his arms, her lips lifted to his. Lee Dawes stooped to pick up his luggage, anger pouring a wicked stream through him.

CHAPTER THREE

The eastbound transcontinental of the OR&N moved swiftly out of The Dalles shortly before noon the next day, and, watching through the coach window, Lee Dawes received a jumbled impression of this land that was to be the northern terminus of the new railroad. The eastbound slid quickly around the swinging curves, passed the narrows in the river between Big Eddy and Celilo, and *clicked* on by the Indian fishing grounds at Celilo, the falls where in season the Warm Springs, Umatilla, and Yakima tribes came for salmon.

The train crossed the bridge over the Deschutes so swiftly that Lee caught only a glimpse of the water tumbling out of the great defile and broadening quietly into the fork of the Columbia drifting south of Miller's Island. It was this cañon that was to become a railroad battleground, and Lee stared at it until the train had sped on eastward through a brown, barren land.

A boiling tumult was in Lee's mind when he stepped down from the train at windswept Biggs and waited for the Shaniko train to come in on the Columbia Southern line. He took a quick turn around the big depot, the eternal sand shifting against his ankles and making a strange, *hissing* sound as it moved with ceaseless energy. Across the street from the depot were some weathered shacks, one of them with a tall false front bearing the words *WOLFARD'S LUNCHROOM.* A man in an apron came out and began beating a steel triangle to attract the attention of the travelers. Lee moved toward the lunchroom, impelled less by hunger than restlessness.

He bought a ham sandwich and a cup of coffee and, since the room was filled, stepped outside to eat. He considered the twenty-odd people waiting around the depot. Here were the uneasy ones always to be found on the cutting edge of the frontier, twentieth-century counterparts of the covered wagon settlers who had first seen the Columbia from the ridge south of the river. Beyond that ridge lay America's last great empire, the high plateau with its sheepmen, cattle ranchers, and farmers returning to their homes. Here, too, were the newcomers: timber cruisers, drummers, speculators, real estate dealers, town site promoters, homestead locators, and the nondescript vagrants drawn by railroad talk and the promise of easy gain.

Lee returned the empty cup, noting that Hanna Racine was in the crowd. It was the first time he had seen her since they had left the *Inland Belle,* and still she ignored him. Prodded by Stevens's inference that he had been picked for this job because of his way with women, he stepped up to Hanna, and asked: "Can I get you something to eat?"

Her "No" was quick and hung with icicles. Turning from the lunchroom, she crossed the street quickly and disappeared into the depot. A flush of defeat washed over Lee's face. He thought of following her, and immediately knew it would be the wrong move. He had the one trick that he hoped would thaw the chill from her, and he was too old a hand at the game to play his ace too early. His thoughts turned to Deborah Haig, and anger ran through him. Neither Deborah nor Quinn was in sight, and, knowing Mike Quinn, Lee could make a good guess what had happened.

A small man had come from the lunchroom with a mug of coffee. He removed a half-chewed cigar from his lips, took one drink, and immediately spewed it from his mouth. Emptying the cup into the sand, he glanced at Lee and grimaced. "Did you drink the stuff?"

Lee nodded. "It's wet."

"So's the Columbia." The little man returned the mug and came back. Taking a fresh grip on his cigar with worn molars, he nodded westward. "You came to The Dalles on the *Inland Belle,* didn't you?"

"Yes." Lee drew pipe and tobacco from his pocket and, studying the man as he packed the bowl, found that he could not remember him. He was well dressed, and Lee noted that the heels of his expensive boots were built up to increase his height, and that he wore a light-colored Stetson with an extremely high crown. It was a vanity Lee had seen expressed in small men before. He asked: "Were you on the boat?"

"In the main cabin most of the time. Interesting trip through the gorge."

Lee sauntered off, the little man falling into step beside him. They moved slowly to the track side of the depot. Lee felt interest stirring, for he sensed that the other was purposely seeking conversation.

"I've always wondered about this gorge," Lee said, "and some of those marks on the

45

rock. Looks like water had made them, but the Columbia was never that high."

"Perhaps it was. This is an old battleground, my friend. There was a time when the Pacific washed against the Idaho mountains and most of Oregon was nothing more than sludge on its bottom."

Lee looked at him in quick interest. "That's hard to believe."

"Scientists are slowly putting the story together. Probably there were two island masses where we now find the Siskiyous and Blue Mountains. The Cascades and Sierras rose and tore a segment from the sea and pinned it inland. The land kept rising, leaving lakes, but sending most of the water pouring through this gorge." He nodded at the far shore. "There's the evidence you mentioned."

Lee shook his head. "I don't see how anybody, scientist or not, can tell that."

"It's taken a long time to put it together." The little man's cigar had gone out. Now he took a moment to relight it. "Erosions like these, and shells and impresses of plants and animals. They all tell the story to men, like Doctor Condon, who can read it."

"What happened to the lakes?"

"The land had just started its part of the war. Lava poured out of the mountains, filling the lakes and soggy valleys, and the land continued to swell until it shoved the coast line twenty or thirty miles west of where it is now."

"So the sea lost the fight?"

"No. The land couldn't keep up its offensive. It became cold. Ice came down from the north. Mount Mazama collapsed and made Crater Lake. The land sank and the sea rolled in again, back up the Columbia and over the interior. Things were just about the same as when this started."

Lee, knocking his pipe against his heel, thought of Mike Quinn, of their friendship and then a fight, again friendship and a fight. The age-old pattern. Now Quinn was here on the Columbia, and a railroad fight was in the making. He said somberly: "A lot of fights end up that way."

The little man nodded. "That's right. Nothing but bitterness. That's the way it was here. The land made one more try, and threw up the Coast Range. It forced the water out, and held it. The fight was over." He gestured toward the Washington cliffs. "It's all gone now but the traces that tell the story. We have a bright land of golden sunshine left to us with only one shadow falling across it."

"I've heard that somewhere," Lee said

thoughtfully. "It must be a party slogan."

"It could well be," the little man said.

"Do you know Hanna Racine?"

"I know her very well. I saw you talking with her on the boat, and she may have said something like that. It's a favorite expression of mine. What I was trying to show you, my friend, was the cosmic principle of conflict. It's inherent here, the same as everywhere else on the face of the earth." He made an all-inclusive motion. "We quarreled with Britain. The whites fought the Indians. White men fight each other."

"I take it you don't believe in this cosmic principle."

The little man smiled. "That's beside the point. I have to accept conflict whether I like it or not, and I have to fight to gain my ends the same as you or anyone else does." He tossed the frayed cigar butt away. "Violence is brewing again. But, of course, you know that. A railroad man thrives on violence."

It was a shrewd guess. Lee, glancing obliquely at him, wondered whether it was entirely a guess. He said: "I don't know about railroad men thriving on violence. The Oregon Trunk wants to build a railroad, and I want to buy right of way. We are not asking for violence of any kind."

"But you will have it. Harriman's Deschutes Railroad wants to build, too, and there are places in the cañon where you won't be sitting side-by-side and cheering the other on." He nodded toward the incoming train. "I believe this is ours. Perhaps we'll meet again." He moved away.

The Columbia Southern two-car train backed slowly up the spur. Lee waited while the crate imprisoning Willie was brought from the baggage room and put aboard. Then, climbing into the coach, he saw Hanna seated at the other end, the little man standing in the aisle and talking to her. Hanna sat half turned in her seat, and, when she saw Lee, she broke into the little man's words. He nodded, and sat down beside her. Lee, taking a seat in the opposite end of the coach, fancied that she had been afraid he was going to sit with her and that she preferred the little man's company to Lee Dawes's.

Stretching his long legs in front of him, Lee leaned back, his thoughts on the little man and the deliberate way he had struck up a conversation. Whatever the man's object was, Lee at least had discovered he was a close friend of Hanna Racine's, and Hanna believed in the people's railroad.

It took most of the afternoon to reach

Shaniko. Lee stared through the window while the little train toiled up the steep grade of Spanish Hollow and wound along the cañon until it reached the plateau. There it rolled with increased speed through the wheat fields, on through Wasco, Moro, Grass Valley, and Kent, and up the steeper climb to Shaniko. There was the sharpness of the sun upon the earth, upon the young grain bulging now with the growth-urge of spring, and then the occasional flow of shadow as a cloud crossed the sun. The long run of the Cascades lay westward — blue in the distance except for white, sharp-peaked Hood and Jefferson. As the train approached Shaniko, grain fields gave way to the forlorn emptiness of the sagebrush desert.

Lee saw now that he had ridden the length of the Columbia Southern, that Stevens had been right when he had said that this was not a feasible route into the interior. The grade was too steep. And he saw more clearly than before how important was the Deschutes cañon — twisting a dozen miles to the west — as an avenue for draining the great pool of wealth held in central Oregon.

Lee, closing his eyes, let his mind drift, the *click* of wheels on rails a steady rhythm distantly heard. There had been his boyhood in St. Paul when, as the oldest of ten children, he had sometimes wondered why he had grown so big when there had been so little to eat. Those were the lean, hard years when his schooling had been spotty, when his father's sawmill check had never been quite enough, and when his own boyhood years had gone mostly into adding a few extra dollars to the family income.

It had been no more possible for Lee to remain there and fall into the prevailing rut of life than it would have been for Jim Hill to surrender the Deschutes cañon without a fight. Hill had been an important figure in St. Paul, and, to Lee Dawes, a hero. Born with fiddle feet and a rebellious heart, Lee had resented his father's stern rule and heartless beatings, and had finally run away.

In his late teens Lee had made a swing through the logging camps of northern Minnesota, on into the wheat belt, and finally, in his early twenties, he had met Mike Quinn. It had been a strange blend of friendship and rivalry that had kept the pair together. Quinn's background had been much like Lee's. There was the same urgency in him to see over the next hill, the same passion for excitement, good liquor, and ardent women, and at times it had taken surprisingly little to make them fight for or against each other.

They had drifted south together, across
the Gulf and the Caribbean, and then to
Nicaragua, where there was talk of a canal
to be constructed by the United States.
There had been fun shared, hopes and
miseries pooled, and there had been differ-
ences. Quinn had taken a curvaceous
señorita from Lee in Nicaragua, and then
had not wanted her. In Panama, Lee had
smashed a loud brag down Quinn's throat,
wrecked a *cantina,* and ended up in jail.

Returning to the States, Quinn had landed
a job as a trouble-shooting special agent
with the Union Pacific, and had taken Lee
on as his assistant. But it was not in Lee to
serve well under Mike Quinn. And, too, Jim
Hill had always been something of an idol
to him. So, when the opportunity came, Lee
had gone over to the Hill interests in time
to participate in the North Bank fight.

Quinn accused Lee of treason, of quitting
the Harriman line when his loyalty was
needed. Then the final break had come over
a waitress in Vancouver. The police had
stopped the fight, but there had been no
handshake after it was over. Lee had not
seen Quinn from that moment until the
Inland Belle was pulling into The Dalles,
and, remembering the way Deborah Haig
had gone into Quinn's arms, Lee swore and

felt a feral hatred travel along his spine. She was the first woman he had ever seriously wanted, and again it was Mike Quinn who had appeared to challenge him.

While Lee waited at the Shaniko depot for Willie to be taken out of the baggage car, he recalled vaguely that this was the end of steel for a rich hinterland. Stage lines radiated into the interior. Freighters laboriously brought the means of life over two hundred miles of desert to Silver Lake.

Shaniko, the biggest wool-shipping point in the United States, was little more than a scattering of business buildings and shacks. Warehouses and shipping corrals were strung along the track, and a block or so away was the heart of the town — stores, hotels, and eating places. All around lay Shaniko Flat, a far-stretching sweep of sagebrush plateau, and, looking beyond the town, Lee could see no sign of habitation.

Lee let Willie loose from the crate that held him prisoner on the long ride from The Dalles. Willie pawed at Lee's leg, made a darting run after an imaginary rabbit, yipping enthusiastically in his freedom, and racing back to Lee, sat down and yawned loudly.

Laughing, Lee scratched a floppy ear, and said with some regret: "Tomorrow you'll have a pretty girl for a mistress. Your luck is changing, Willie."

Finding a butcher shop, Lee bought some meat, and tied Willie in the area behind the L-shaped Columbia Southern Hotel. Then he carried his luggage into the lobby, which was large and attractive, a staircase rising to the second floor, warmth from the huge stove filling the room.

"When does the next stage leave for Madras?" Lee asked at the desk.

"You'll take the Bend stage. It pulls out about eight."

Glancing at the register, Lee saw that neither Quinn nor Deborah Haig was here. They might be at the Shaniko Hotel, but the Columbia Southern was the larger and more desirable. If he'd judged Deborah right, she'd be here if she were in town. Likely, he thought, they would come on the next afternoon's train.

The urgency of responsibility warned Lee to take the stage, to get on to Hanna's place as quickly as he could, but the temptation to wait another day was strong. He could still get to the Racine Ranch as soon as Quinn could. Besides, Quinn had evidently been in the country. If he was the one who was buying right of way for the Harriman line, he'd have bought it long before this, if he could. Besides, twenty-four hours would give Hanna more time to forget she was angry.

Standing there at the desk, Lee debated it with himself, thinking of a dozen reasons why he should stay and none why he should go on. The desire to see Deborah again was a burning flame in him, but he reserved decision until after he'd eaten. Turning left, he crossed the lobby to the dining room. He had just started to eat when the little man with whom he had talked at Biggs came in and sat down at his table.

"It struck me I failed to introduce myself," the man said, a smile breaking across his high-boned, rosy face. "I'm Cyrus P. Jepson. Perhaps you've heard of the Jepson City town site east of Bend."

"Don't believe I have," Lee said. "I'm Lee Dawes, but you know that by now."

Jepson gave his order and, drawing a cigar from his pocket, slipped it into his mouth. "Why, yes, Hanna told me your name. I presume you're going on south."

"That's right." This was another deliberate contact, and Lee wondered if it had grown out of the man's conversation on the train with Hanna.

"A fine country around Bend," Jepson said, blowing out a long plume of smoke.

55

"Get the sagebrush off and the water on it, and it'll grow anything. Bend will be a town of ten thousand people when the railroad reaches it, and I sincerely believe that my own town will rival it when the railroad is built across the desert."

"You think a line will be built east from Bend?"

Jepson took the cigar from his mouth, large eyes pinned on Lee. "Why, yes. It has to, if the products destined for the big Eastern markets are to be shipped by the shortest route to that market."

The waitress had brought Jepson's plate, but the little man did not touch it. He was watching Lee, studying his lean face, the set of his square jaw, and he seemed to find it hard to make up his mind about something. Finally he said: "You've heard of the people's railroad?"

Lee nodded as he reached for the bread. Cyrus Jepson was tipping his hand, and Lee, not wanting to frighten the man into silence, merely said: "I hear it's to go on the ballot."

"That's right. Big men are behind it, Dawes, men like C.E.S. Wood. A bill was passed by the legislature providing for the people to vote on a proposed constitutional amendment. If passed, it will authorize the construction of publicly owned railroads,

56

and it will be passed because the big railroad men have forgotten Oregon too long."

"We'll have two railroads into central Oregon before long," Lee pointed out.

"Promises," Jepson scoffed. "Nothing more, and they're being made to defeat this measure. Besides, this isn't the route a railroad should follow. What we need is an east-west road crossing the Cascades from the Willamette Valley, perhaps Salem, and running across the state to Vale. Through Jepson City, Mister Dawes."

"I see," Lee said amiably. John F. Stevens had mentioned a third interest. He had spoken of tricks that did not square with the customary actions of the Harriman people. Here, across the table from Lee, might well be this third party who wanted neither Hill nor Harriman to build into central Oregon. "What are you getting at?"

"A special agent for a railroad outfit has influence, but he runs big risks for a small salary. To an outsider, it doesn't look smart."

Lee scooted back his chair. He said gently, a gentleness that would have warned a man who knew him better: "So I might make a little money for myself by selling out the Oregon Trunk to a man who stands to profit by the people's railroad. Is that what you're saying, Jepson?"

"You put things bluntly, Mister Dawes," Jepson murmured.

Lee rose. "In other words, you figure you'll snarl up both outfits, so they'll withdraw and leave you to swing the people's railroad any direction you want. It's no good, Jepson. Outfits the size of Hill's and Harriman's don't quit like that."

Jepson had placed both hands palm down on the table. He said: "There are a few tricks you haven't seen, Dawes. And there is such a thing as a railroad serving the people. That's not a popular doctrine, but it's the way I believe." Jepson's smile was soft, almost cherubic. "I propose to remove the shadow that is falling across our bright land."

"You'll have to have taller boot heels than you're wearing now," Lee said, and left the dining room.

For a time Lee stood on the sidewalk, watching the flow of the crowd, pulling so fiercely on his pipe that the smoke burned his tongue. It was nearly dark now, with the last light of a dying sun leaving the cold, wind-touched earth. Lee felt tension grow in him. There was more to this game than he had thought.

Jepson had put no direct offer into words; yet a bribe was there for the taking. He thought of Hanna, and of Jepson's influence with her, and a scowl furrowed his forehead. Her property was vital, then, to three parties instead of two. She was probably in Shaniko waiting for the stage. He'd be on that stage with her, and he'd have an opportunity to talk. If she would talk! In either case, it was not the time to talk business. Not while she was angry with him, and before he had a chance to play the ace he was counting on so much.

Another idea had been building in Lee's mind. If she would not sell, he could buy the property around her, box her in, keep her from selling to someone else. Jepson had mentioned a few tricks Lee hadn't seen. All right, there were some tricks Jepson and Mike Quinn hadn't seen. Lee Dawes had a checkbook, and John Stevens had said the sky was the limit.

Lee had to go on tonight. Reluctant as he was to miss seeing Deborah tomorrow, he had to be at Hanna's place in the morning, to see her neighbors as soon as possible. If necessary, he'd buy every ranch between Madras and Crooked River.

A man hurried out of the alley behind the hotel, and came down the street toward Lee. "Mister, ain't that your little black dog tied back there in the alley?" he called.

"Yes. Why?"

"You don't have no dog. That's all. Ken Villard's big bulldog came along and chewed hell out of him."

Panic seized Lee. Now he didn't have any ace to play. He wheeled past the man, racing in long strides into the alley. It was dark, and he couldn't remember hearing the racket of a dogfight. Maybe the man was wrong. Maybe it wasn't Willie. Maybe. . . .

"Over here!" a man called. "Right here against this wall."

That was all Lee knew, for something fell on him, consciousness went out of him, and he spilled forward.

CHAPTER FOUR

There were brittle, dangerous thoughts in Lee Dawes's mind as the black fog rolled away, incoherent and vague impressions stirring a numbed brain. His body was cold. His head ached. He felt the impress of damp earth under him, and it was as if a wet sponge was mopping his face. He heard the run of talk from the street, a man's whistle, the *clatter* of dishes from the nearby hotel kitchen. A *whine* beat against his ears, then he discovered Willie over him, and realized that the sponge was the dog's tongue on his face.

For a time Lee sat with his back against the hotel wall, an arm around the dog to reassure him, trying to make sense from what had happened, and failing. Cigar-smoking, poetry-making little Cyrus P. Jepson had made his try at bribery with, it seemed, an effective substitute in mind.

Recalling that the stage was to leave at

8:00 P.M., Lee scrambled to his feet, stood still until the nausea passed, then untied the dog and led him out of the alley and into the lobby. "The stage gone yet?" he asked.

The clerk nodded, pointing to the big wall clock that showed a quarter past eight. "Rolled out on time," he said.

It had to be Jepson — and perhaps Hanna Racine. For some reason they had wanted to keep him off that stage. Lee left the hotel and drifted along the street, a sour humiliation in him. He'd be in Shaniko until the next stage left, regardless of the decision he'd made.

Telling Willie to stay outside, Lee stepped into a saloon, and loitered over a drink, bitterness and acid washing through him. He stood at the bar for a time, thinking of ways to checkmate the move, and finding none that offered much promise.

The low roof of the saloon dropped until it seemed almost to touch the barman's oily, slick-haired head. There were two tables along the inside wall, occupied but silent except for an occasional murmur of talk, the whisper of shuffled cards, the *click* of poker chips. A man shoved back his chair, leaned toward the spittoon, and spat. These things Lee noted absently, making a faint curtain of motion and sound in the back of his mind. Then the din of angry controversy broke across his thoughts, and he looked along the bar.

"You *hombres* are too dad-burned big for your britches, Bull."

A tall, angry man stood there, a bottle of soda pop in his hands, a man whose tallness and too-small clothes gave him a grotesque appearance. His hairy wrists hung well below his coat sleeves; his pants legs were high above bony ankles. He pulled at his black beard, raised a hand to tug at a sailboat ear, and the badgered fury in his narrowed eyes showed that he was close to the exploding point.

Four men made a half circle around him. Freighters, Lee guessed. The man the tall one watched and called Bull was both thick and broad of body, and there was about his knobby face a thoroughly ugly look, a savage appetite for cruelty.

"You sure look dangerous, Highpockets," Bull said in a feigned tone of fright. "Hell, you don't need to get mad just because I said the stage line was getting so hard up for drivers they put a giraffe on the box."

"He's a camel, Bull," another said. "Don't drink for seven days, and then goes after sarsaparilla like he was dying of thirst."

"Forty-rod would singe his whiskers," a

third one jeered.

Lee had seen this pattern build into savage fighting more than once in frontier towns like Shaniko; sometimes merely for crude amusement, but often for a more deadly purpose. Even if the tall one was a good fighting man, he would not last long against these odds.

The lanky Highpockets set his bottle carefully on the bar. He regarded his tormenters for a moment with level eyes, and suddenly broke into action so swiftly that he caught the others flat-footed. Seizing two men by their shirt collars, he shoved them hard against the big man and, as suddenly reversing the order, jerked them in the opposite direction and sent them spinning to the floor.

It was a display of disdainful nerve and great strength that reached Lee, and instantly enlisted his sympathy with the tall man. Then Bull bellowed — "You're gonna get all you asked for, you damned beanpole!" — and something clicked in Lee. It was the same voice he had heard in the alley the instant before he had been slugged.

Lee peeled off his coat and tossed it on the bar, just as Bull drove a fist at Highpockets and the other three closed in on him. Lee grabbed the first man by the shoulder, pulled him around, and drove a short, turning fist squarely to his exposed jaw. It was a knockout punch, the man going down in a curling drop.

There was a mêlée around Lee, then, as men scrambled away from the card tables. For all of Highpockets's stringiness, he was a good man to fight beside. He drove Bull back, spun, and, whipping a fist into a man's stomach, blasted the wind from him and knocked him cold with a second punch.

In a matter of seconds the fight changed complexion entirely, with Lee finding himself facing Bull and trading brain-jarring punches with him, while Highpockets battered the remaining freighter across the saloon in a fast retreat.

A card table went over, chips spilling and rolling across the floor. A spittoon slid against the bar with a dull *bong.* The barman, eyeing the fight with jaded interest, said sourly: "That damned Boston Bull is just bound to kick up a fight."

There were no rules in Boston Bull's fighting code. He came in fast, only to be rocked back on his heels when Lee's fist in his stomach brought air gushing from his lungs. He went back, dropping the attack until breath was in him again. Lee bore in after him, feinting, shifting, trying for his head,

65

but he found no hole in the big man's defense. Then, without warning, Bull reversed his tactics, and charged forward, great hands outstretched.

Lee refused to give ground. The freighter tried to knee him in the crotch and, failing in that maneuver, drove a thumb at Lee's right eye. Lee turned his head, took the prodding thumb on his temple, and felt anger spurt through the pain. They were together now, straining, neither able to get in an effective blow, and Lee, bent by the other's greater weight, brought his head upward against the big man's chin.

There was a *click* of teeth, and blood streamed down the freighter's sweating chin as the tip of his tongue was sheared off. It was barroom fighting, wicked and ruthless, and Lee Dawes thrilled to it, all the bitterness he had felt from the moment he'd seen Mike Quinn at The Dalles now finding expression in every blow he smashed into Boston Bull's big body.

A heel ground against Lee's left foot. Pain shot up his leg. Shifting weight to his right leg, he forced Bull back against the bar, heard a grunt and a choked oath. Then he got his forearm against the man's windpipe, and heaved, the steady, hard pressure turning Bull's knobby face first red and then white while his fists beat at Lee with no more than a faint sting in them.

"You got him!" Highpockets yelled. "Bust his neck, partner. Kick him in the belly. He ain't never been licked in Shaniko before. Go on . . . !"

"He ain't out yet, skinny," another man cut in.

Lee stepped back, and with his weight released, the freighter bounced forward, bloody chin exposed. There was a sharp, wicked *crack* that ran the length of the room as Lee's fist met that chin, and there was a new champion in Shaniko. Boston Bull sprawled full out, a great, motionless bulk, his face a patchwork of mottled bruises.

Lee ran a sleeve across his forehead, heard the barman say: "You boys have had your fun. Go on now. Drift."

Boston Bull's three companions were on their feet again, not quite believing what they saw, the desire for revenge a bright wickedness in their eyes. Lee pulled into his coat and moved toward the door. Following, Highpockets stopped him on the sidewalk and offered his hand.

"I'm Highpockets Magoon. Sure glad to know you, and thanks."

"Lee Dawes." He gave the tall man's hand a hard grip, their eyes locking. "You're long as a wash line, friend, but you don't fight like one."

Highpockets grinned with the compliment. "You're sure a fighting man from a way back yourself." He sobered. "That Boston Bull is a bad one, Mister Dawes. He won't forget this. Don't never turn your back to him or his outfit if you meet up with them again."

"What was the ruckus over?"

Highpockets thrust bony hands into his pants pockets, and chuckled. "Nothing. That is, nothing to speak of. They wanted some fun, and I'm a good one to hooraw. I don't smoke. I don't chew. I don't gamble. I don't drink nothing but soda pop."

"You're a stage driver?"

Highpockets nodded. "Yeah, but I'm getting a week off, starting today."

There was a full moon in the black sky, webbed over with a tattered cloud. Its thin light spilled into the streets, glinting on the puddled water standing in the wheel ruts, building deeper recesses of shadow in the darkness. It was characteristic of Shaniko that the racket of the saloon fight had failed to draw a crowd of the curious. Save for the lighted windows and a man's drunken singing farther along the block, the town seemed empty.

"Is there any way to get to Madras tonight?" Lee asked.

"Well, now, they got some of them automobiles around, but they're all off somewhere. Hanna Racine got one soon as she hopped off the train, and went foggin' home. Reckon there's no way of getting to Madras in a hurry, but there is slow. You wait here." Highpockets wheeled away and went down the street in long strides.

Lee stared after the tall man. So Hanna had been in a big enough hurry to hire an automobile to get home. Cyrus Jepson had been determined to keep Lee off the stage. And Boston Bull had a hand in it. There was some satisfaction in knowing that Bull had paid for his part. It would be a long day before he would get whiskey past that mutilated tongue, and even a longer one before his foul-mouthed cursing would return to its former efficiency. Standing here on the boardwalk, Lee thought swiftly of this night's happenings. He still could not see the design of its strange pattern, but one thing was clear. Hanna had been in a tremendous hurry, and the realization of that fact raised a new sense of urgency in Lee.

A small dog raced across an intersection down the street, and in response to Lee's sharp whistle Willie bounded up. Lee crossed to the hotel to get his grips, and a few minutes later Highpockets pulled up with a team of bays hitched to a buggy. He called: "Climb in, mister, and hang on!"

The light, spirited team left Shaniko on the run, the buggy swaying and *rattling* over the rough road. The lights of the town dropped quickly behind, and they raced on into the pit-black night.

"I'm putting you to a lot of trouble, Highpockets," Lee said. "You can name your own price when we get to Madras."

"No price, mister, after what you done for me. Now don't get the notion I'm nosey, but you've got railroad written all over you. Hill or Harriman?"

"Oregon Trunk. Beyond that your guess is as good as mine." Lee paused, and then asked: "You know a big Irishman named Mike Quinn?"

"You bet. Saw him just this morning when I brought the stage in. Him and that dark-haired filly he's been running with was in one of them steam autos, stuck in Cow Cañon. I pulled 'em out. The crazy galoot said they'd drove all night getting here from The Dalles. Crossed the river on Free Bridge, and I'll bet they got a dad-burned good shaking up. Him and the girl ride the stage a lot, together and separate, which is how come I give him a hand."

Again Lee had the feeling of being the end man in a game of crack-the-whip. He clenched his big fists, recalling the subtle way Deborah Haig had felt him out about John Stevens. It was likely, he thought sourly, that she had reported what little she had learned to Quinn, and it had been enough to start him on a wild night chase across rough, broken country. They were hours ahead of him, and so was Hanna Racine, and Lee was looking more and more like a blundering fool.

They were still running swiftly across the seemingly endless rolling Shaniko Flats. Periodically the moon crawled out from behind ragged black clouds, lighting the lonely sweeps of bunchgrass and sage that somehow seemed timeless, and frightening. Now and then a strident howl sounded from some distant rock point.

"Coyotes," Highpockets said. "That one could sure stand tuning. Ever been in Bend?"

"No."

"Great town and great people. Farewell Bend they used to call it when the pioneer wagons left the river there. Gonna be a big town if it gets a railroad. Got a right lively

Commercial Club down there already. The way they're boosting it, they'll make it the met . . . metrop . . . the dad-burnedest, biggest town in eastern Oregon. Take fellers like Doc Coe and Clyde McKay . . . they want a real town, and my money's on 'em getting one."

"Any other towns that might grow?"

"Lot of 'em think they will. Prineville, that's the county seat of Crook County, and Redmond, on this side of Bend. There's Laidlaw. Madras. Shucks, to hear them tell it, they'll all be big towns."

"Jepson City?"

"Way out in the desert east of Bend. A few buildings and tents, and a couple miles of stakes. Jepson bet on a road coming east across the mountains, and, if he don't get it, he'll be sitting in the sagebrush with the jack rabbits. You've met up with Jepson?"

"Met him in Biggs."

"He's a funny critter. He can talk your leg right off about the way this country got made. Kind of sings about it, but he ain't the kind of man it takes to build a town in this country. Leastwise, I don't think so. Now that go-getting Bend bunch is different. Say, they put a party on in the Pilot Butte Inn one night that was a party. One of 'em was getting married, and it called for

72

enough likker to wash Pilot Butte right off the map.

"Had bottles arranged on the table so you could grab 'em from any position, including a prone one. One feller stepped outside, picked up a hose, and started wetting everybody down. Another gent crawled under the table, and every time he poked his head out he got sprayed with seltzer water. Had a big cake iced with gooey stuff an inch thick. Before the party wound up, one feller picks the cake up, and spreads it all over his neighbor's face."

Highpockets chuckled. "Yep, they're live wires. A couple of 'em got about halfway down Wall Street when they found a young wildcat asleep in front of a store. Reckon he'd just et . . . to be sleeping along so peaceful. Anyhow, they picked him up and fetched him a piece, and, when they got tired toting him, they packed him into a friend's house and put him into bed with the friend. Well, when the cat woke up along about dawn, he was hungry again, and there was a nice hunk of back meat waiting for him, so he helped himself." Highpockets laughed and slapped a leg. "Well, sir, next day them fellers had to come back and shingle the roof where their friend went through it."

They rode in silence for a time, the horses keeping an even fast pace, the blackness unscarred by light until a campfire gleamed ahead of them. "Somebody live there?" Lee asked.

"Nope. Just a freighter's sagebrush fire. Somebody about like Bull, except he wouldn't be so dad-burned ornery."

"Bull goes to Bend?"

"Goes to Jepson City part of the time. Fact is, he's freighted for Jepson ever since Jepson staked out the town site. Jepson's got a store that takes care of what few homesteaders settled out there."

"This country around here isn't worth much, is it?"

"Just for stock. Gumbo mud that'd mire a snipe in winter, and dust in summers that'd choke a mole. Don't get much rain. When it does, the bottom falls out of the road. The wind she blows and blows. Feller back there a piece dug himself a well once, and I'll be dad-burned if the wind didn't come up and blow the land away. Yes, sir, left that well sticking up in the air. Sure was a funny sight."

Lee grinned. "I'll bet it was."

"It's a fact. It was hard water, but it wasn't hard enough to stay there. Over in Antelope they'd been toughing out a dry spell. One windy night they snuck over and blasted it. Got themselves a dandy little rain." He spat over the wheel. "Good thing it was winding, or they'd 'a' drowned sure."

It seemed hours later to Lee when they started down the wicked steepness of Cow Cañon. They emerged from the narrow, winding passage, and passed Haight's Station. Coming now onto the floor of the narrow valley, the buggy picked up speed.

"Look over there to the right. That big gap is where Trout Creek cuts down to the river. Harriman's Deschutes Railroad will pull out of the cañon about there."

Lee straightened, fully awake and interested. "How far to the Columbia?"

"Seventy miles. Eighty maybe. If you're going to have anything to do with building that railroad, you'll have to practice bending your bones. About the only way you can look is up. The river's so crooked in some places that the trout they pull out are shaped like corkscrews."

"I won't be doing any of the building," Lee said dryly, "so that won't worry me."

Under the seat, Willie stirred in his slumber, and laid his muzzle across Lee's foot. Remembering the distance he had traveled since he had passed the mouth of the Deschutes, Lee had a more stirring impression of the magnitude of the job ahead of the Oregon Trunk. Seventy or eighty miles of vast cañon that was to be disputed foot by foot, in addition to the natural problems inherent in such terrain.

"Where's the Racine Ranch?"

"That where you're heading? It's past Madras. Part way to Trail Crossing on Crooked River. I'll get another team in Madras and take you on."

"I've put you out enough."

"Nope," Highpockets said emphatically. "You stuck with me to the end, and, if you hadn't, them ornery devils would have made mincemeat out of my handsome mug. Never would have looked the same again. Besides, I'm hungry for some of Hanna's cooking. She's been gone for quite a spell. I used to go out there and eat with her every week or so."

"Gone? Where to?"

"Oh, Portland. Salem some of the time. She was down there when the legislature was meeting, and I guess she did a lot of good getting that people's railroad thing passed."

This, then, might be the reason for Mike Quinn's hurry. If Hanna had been away, Quinn would have had no opportunity to see her, and, hearing that she was on her way home, he'd hurried south from The Dalles. But it still gave Lee no explanation of Hanna's haste.

"Is Hanna pretty friendly with Jepson?" he asked.

"Not what you'd call thick, but they see this people's railroad the same way, so they work together on that. Hanna fell heir to a lot of notions from her daddy, but she's got her heart in it, too. Herb Racine was an old friend of mine. Someday they'll get the man that bushwacked him, and I'll sure dance at his hanging."

"Got any notion who did it?"

Highpockets didn't say anything for a time. Then he cleared his throat. "I got a notion, but I ain't for hanging a man on a notion. Herb had a way of making enemies. He'd speak his piece, hell or high water, and he'd tromp on the toes of his best friend if he figured it was the right thing to do. He was coming home from Redmond one night, and somebody drilled him from the rocks when he was coming across Crooked River. They found his body right in the middle of the bridge."

"I heard he was pretty set in his ideas about the railroads."

"Well, I think he had a good idea. He wanted the state to build the railroads, see-

ing as Harriman wasn't doing it. He figured
there should be one crossing the Cascades,
maybe come up the Santiam and go on
through Bend and Jepson City. It'd hook up
with the spur that comes into Vale, so our
freight would go right on east over the
Union Pacific. Anyhow, that's how come
Jepson and Hanna got tied up with it.
They're against a north-south road, and
Hanna's got a fistful of aces. If your outfit . . . or Harriman's either . . . is gonna
cross Crooked River, you're gonna buy a
right of way through Hanna's place."

"We can condemn a right of way," Lee
said dryly.

"Yeah." Highpockets chuckled. "But can
two railroads do it? Maybe you're a little
worried about which one is gonna get that
right of way. Another thing is the ranchers
around her place look to her to call the turn.
She's a smart girl, and her neighbors know
it. Start condemning, and you might kick
up a piece of real trouble."

"You say she's got a lot of influence?" Lee
asked with quick interest.

"Plenty. Her neighbors will sell right of
way if she does, and, if she won't, they
won't."

A knot tied itself around Lee's stomach.
Gone was his neat plan for buying up the

property around her, boxing her in, and forcing her to come to his terms. He cursed softly to himself. The only thing left was to argue with a head-strong girl, and Lee had a feeling Hanna Racine could take care of herself in any kind of argument.

Sometime close to dawn they wheeled into Madras. Highpockets rattled the door of a livery stable until a sleepy-eyed hostler came to open it. With the bays stabled and grained, and a fresh team hitched to the buggy, they rolled on. They were in a more heavily settled country now, and, as they spun on south, the first light of dawn spread across the earth, lighting it with alternate patches of red and purple shadow.

"We're almost there," Highpockets grunted. "Just about in time for breakfast, and, the way my tapeworm is hollering for fodder, I sure could use some."

They left the road, turning westward toward the river, and presently, ahead, Lee saw the ranch buildings — a two-story house with a row of naked poplars along the front, a barn, corrals, and a scattering of outbuildings. Smoke lifted from the kitchen chimney, and, as Highpockets pulled the horses to a stop in front of the house, Lee was impressed with the neatness and care everywhere so evident.

The kitchen door opened, and Hanna Racine stood there, a slight, cool figure in a cotton dress. She gave no greeting, her eyes moving from Highpockets to Lee as if he stood a great distance from her.

Unabashed, Highpockets chuckled. "Back there about Madras my stomach collapsed. Does it danged near every morning. Sure hope that's biscuit flour I see on your nose, girl."

Smiling reluctantly, Hanna came across the yard, still without greeting Lee, and he knew that the events on the *Inland Belle* had hurt her woman's pride as badly as he had feared. Then there was movement under his feet, and an awakening Willie scrambled forward and stood with his forepaws on the side of the buggy. The dog yawned elaborately, and began to wag his tail, his head cocked, one ear up.

"Why, Lee Dawes! How did you get him?"

"Stole him," he said amiably, "and rode all night so I could keep ahead of the lynchers and deliver him to you personally. Now that you have him, they can hang me."

The tension ebbing, Lee swung to the ground, and, after a moment of forced soberness, Hanna laughed. "Of course, I believe that. We hang dog stealers down here just like we hang horse thieves. Willie, we

80

have trees, if you like junipers." Willie had already made that discovery and dashed away. Hanna turned her gaze to Lee, her smile small and stiff. "You've earned your breakfast, Mister Dawes. The boys are eating, so you'll have to put your horses away, Highpockets." She nodded at Lee. "If you'll come with me, I'll show you where to wash."

There was a basin, a bucket of water, and a roller towel on the back porch. Hanna motioned to them, and went on into the kitchen where an Indian woman was busy at a huge range. Lee washed, and was combing his hair when Highpockets came from the barn.

"Hey, Hanna!" Highpockets called through the screen door. "Did you go and buy yourself one of them dad-burned autos?"

"No."

"Then who owns that rig in the barn?"

The answer was drowned in a *clatter* of dishes. Highpockets led Lee through the door into the kitchen. Five men were seated at the long table, four of them members of Hanna's crew.

Lee paused just inside the door, his eyes riveted on the thick-shouldered man seated across the table from him. "Well, I'll be

81

damned," Lee breathed. "I suppose you'll be popping out of my beer next, Quinn."

CHAPTER FIVE

The ranch hands paused in their eating, and Mike Quinn looked up with quick interest, a look of perverse satisfaction in his eyes. There was a moment of silence, in which somebody's knife *clattered* loudly as it dropped from his hand to the table. Then Hanna, as if sensing the need to break this sharp unpredictable moment, said: "So you two know each other."

Quinn's face relaxed into a sour grin. "We'd ought to." Looking at Lee, he added: "Looks like you tangled with a grizzly, Dawes."

"Something like that," Lee said.

"Sit down." Hanna motioned toward two empty places. "I did make biscuits, High-pockets."

Lee sank into the chair, glancing obliquely at Quinn, who had sobered, the old sense of frustration knifing through him. Across from him, Hanna was bending now to pour Highpockets's coffee, the set of her finely chiseled features telling Lee that Quinn had probably gotten nowhere with her. She filled Lee's cup, and in the steaming fragrance of the coffee was a sweeter scent that he knew was hers, and his senses stirred.

"What did you do with your stage, Highpockets?" she asked.

"Taking a week off." Highpockets forked half a dozen sausages onto his plate. "Gonna sit right here till it's over."

"Do you want to break the outfit?" Hanna asked with mock concern.

"Nope. Just get full. Eat up, Lee. Sure makes Hanna mad when a man just pecks at his grub like you're doing."

"Not all men are as thoughtful as you," Hanna said coolly.

Lee's gaze touched hers, and he felt the rebuke. He lowered his eyes to his plate, knowing that he would have to pay for his lack of gallantry on the *Inland Belle.*

"We're sure losing ground this morning," one of the hands said. "Takes six months to raise a hog and five minutes for Highpockets to eat it. You ought to ride over to Bend and let Doc Coe look you over. If you ain't got a hollow leg, I'll miss my guess."

"Never mind, Chris," Hanna said.

"I ain't minding him at all." Highpockets

serenely helped himself to the rest of the sausage. "A gent with a puny appetite like his ain't much good on a ranch. Right nice of you to pension him off, Hanna."

Mary, the Indian girl, took the platter to the kitchen and brought it back filled. Conversation lagged, largely because Highpockets was too busy eating to talk. Lee noted the pleasantness of the big room, planned for utility with big windows for winter light and summer air, the large table so well supplied, the buffet running along the brightly papered inside wall. It was, he thought, like its slight-figured mistress, fundamental and stripped of useless refinements, yet wholesome and warm and appealing.

The buckaroos left the table as soon as they had finished eating, and there were only the newcomers, with Hanna and Quinn, at the table. Quinn had pushed back his chair and was smoking. Watching him, Lee sensed the amusement that was in the man, the mockery. Irritation stretched Lee's nerves as he remembered that the big Irishman had beaten him here, had beaten him to Deborah Haig. Curiosity stirred in Lee, then, as he remembered Highpockets saying Deborah had been in the automobile with Quinn in Cow Cañon.

Regretfully Highpockets shoved back from the table. "Sure is a hard decision, Hanna, leaving all that good grub. What time's dinner?"

"You can have it now."

"Why, I guess I'll just take me an appetizer." He reached for another sausage, and popped it into his mouth as he went out.

Hanna looked at Lee, her eyes questioning. "Quinn's a Harriman man, so, Dawes, I suppose you belong to Hill."

Lee had filled his pipe, and took a moment to light it. "I work for the Oregon Trunk. I don't belong to any man."

The girl shrugged. "I've been trying to tell Quinn this since late last night when I got home, and I'll repeat it for your benefit. I'm selling no right of way through my place. Neither are my neighbors. That's why I hurried home from Shaniko. I haven't been here for several months, and, when I heard rumors that Hill and Harriman were finally moving, I knew I'd better get back and talk to my neighbors again. I did, and found that I had nothing to worry about. They haven't changed, and neither have I. So, gentlemen, unless you want to help Mary with the dishes, the meeting's over."

"She does hold to that word no." Quinn

86

grinned wryly. "And her neighbors use it so much it gets monotonous. The Oregon Trunk won't buy a right of way through here, my friend. So, unless you want to help with the dishes. . . ."

"I have two dishcloths, Mister Quinn." Hanna looked at Lee sharply. "You are working for Jim Hill, aren't you?"

"The Oregon Trunk."

Quinn snorted. "Hill isn't fooling anybody."

"He isn't fooling me." Hanna leaned across the table. "Mister Dawes, this talk about Jim Hill being an empire builder simply makes me sick . . . unless you mean Hill's own empire! He comes with blandishments and stays to fill his pockets. Look what he did in Spokane. Look at his terminal rate scheme. You're a railroad man, so you know that we pay more freight on goods from the East than they do on the coast. The railroads justify it by claiming they have to meet ocean rates, which the Panama Canal will make possible. Do you know anything about the finances of Hill's Great Northern?"

"Well, I. . . ."

"If you did, you wouldn't want to admit it. They're so afraid of revealing their profits by declaring them in dividends that they spend millions in expansion to cover them up. That might well be the very reason James J. Hill is now interested in building a railroad up the Deschutes. If he is."

Quinn was grinning broadly. "That's right, Miss Racine. That's exactly right."

She whirled on him. "You have no room to talk, Quinn. Your Ed Harriman is cut from the same cloth. What about the public lands investigation now on? Land grants that went to the Oregon and California Railroad, and were never opened for settlement as was specified in the grants. When Harriman took it over, he withdrew it all from public sale. The idea behind those grants was to bring settlers into the country, but much of what was sold went to vested interests at high prices and in large tracts." Her eyes flashed. "Don't spring the public benefactor argument on me, gentlemen."

Lee winked at Quinn, amused that he and Quinn had been maneuvered into an alliance. Quinn winked back as he said: "Miss Racine, you talk like a wobbly."

"It was not my intention." She rose. "Come along. I have another barrel to fire."

She led them through the living room to her office. There was a desk in one corner, without the litter typical of a ranch office, a bookcase set against the wall, a framed photograph of Benham Falls on the Deschutes hanging between two windows. Lee's eyes paused on a framed diploma from the University of Oregon, and he saw that it bore the name of Hanna Rose Racine. There was reason, then, for the sharp argument, the quick mind.

Hanna had stepped around the desk to a large map of the United States tacked to the wall. "Have you heard of the Harriman Fence, Quinn?"

"I've heard the term," Quinn said sourly.

"Dawes, take a look." Placing a finger on Portland, she brought it south along a red line that ran through Salem, Eugene, Ashland, across the state line and on to Roseville, California, a few miles east of Sacramento. "The Southern Pacific, one panel of Harriman's Fence. Seven hundred miles of it." She ran her finger eastward across the Sierras, across Nevada, Utah, and on to Granger, Wyoming. "The second panel, Southern Pacific and Union Pacific. Eight hundred miles or more." She traced the red line westward across Idaho, following the Oregon Short Line and then the OR&N that ran most of the length of Oregon through Baker City, The Dalles, and Hood River. "There it is, back to Portland. Harriman's twenty-five hundred mile fence that very successfully keeps other roads out. You'll notice it forms a triangle, and half of the enclosure that is without railroads is our own Oregon."

Lee dismissed the argument with a wave of the hand. "I wouldn't argue on this point, but the fact remains that you want a railroad. What other sensible means have you got of getting one if the Oregon Trunk doesn't build it?"

Hanna smiled wearily. "I suppose you're taking a backhanded slap at the people's railroad. It's natural that you'd share the industrial giant's contempt for a people's movement, but don't forget these common people are the ones who support the roads you've built."

"Supporting a railroad isn't building it," Lee said, "and, if they did build it, they couldn't run it."

"You underestimate the people, my friend. How do you suppose they did what they've already done here? Your Jim Hill never had to worry about Indians lifting his scalp. Dad did. Paulina and his renegades went through here time after time. Hill never had to join the vigilantes or hang an outlaw, so that Crook County could have law and order. I don't suppose you ever heard of the Crook County Sheep Shooters' Association, or the cattle-sheep war that keeps breaking out. The little people have had to contend with those things, Mister Dawes."

"But building and operating a railroad. . . ."

She spread her hands emphatically. "You don't really know anything about a frontier. It isn't much different here from the way it was a century ago. Who explored it? The fur traders. Men like Peter Skene Ogden and Nathaniel J. Wyeth. Who brought the first wagons and cattle over the McKenzie Pass? Felix Scott. There were miners, sheepmen, cattlemen, freighters, farmers. Little people. They built what is called the Inland Empire, yet you think they can't build and run a railroad."

Temper was crowding Lee now, but he held a tight rein on it. "What you say about the Harriman interests is entirely correct. They've taken their own sweet time about building into the interior of this state, and it's the Oregon Trunk that's moving them now. My company will build your railroad as fast as the job can be done. Your people's line can't even get started until it's voted on a year from next November. Then there are all kinds of problems that will have to be solved . . . financial, legal, getting competent men to build and run it, and keep it in the black . . . something that state-owned roads find hard to do. The smart thing is to leave it to experts. We'll have our line built and running before the organization you hope for can turn a shovelful of dirt."

Hanna had listened carefully, and now she said, a little reluctantly: "Your arguments are sound, Dawes. It did take your company to spur Harriman into action. I admit I lean toward you, if we must have an old line company build our road, but I also know that both companies are interested mainly in controlling Pacific Coast railroading. My section of Oregon has no real meaning to them . . . we're pawns to be moved by the giant chess players. We'll pay terminal rates that will handicap our agriculture, our towns, our settlements. Your bosses had their chance, and we can read what they'll do in the future by the record they've written into the past."

Quinn had tensed, his craggy face granite-hard. "Hill's the power behind the Oregon Trunk, Dawes," he said angrily. "He's trying to block us here to gain concessions on the Portland terminal question. Don't let him fool you, Miss Racine."

Hanna smiled. "You see? You admit that your central Oregon railroad is merely another move in your chess game. I'm sorry, gentlemen, but on a ranch this size, there is a lot of work to do."

Lee never knew whether Highpockets had been listening outside the door or not, but he stomped in now, his bearded face guileless. "I sure do hate to interrupt, Mister Quinn, and I don't know much about these gas buggies, but that there machine of yours has got four tires that look all right, mostly, but on the bottom they're flat as pancakes. Now if you just run on the tops of those tires. . . ."

"Four of them?" Quinn shouted. "Judas!" He shoved Highpockets out of the way and ran across the living room and out of the house.

Highpockets winked at Lee. "Guess I'd better go give him a hand."

"I suspect that the tires are all right." Hanna smiled. "The best recommendation that you could have is for Highpockets to be on your side."

"Somehow we've got off on the wrong foot, Miss Racine," Lee said with a humility that was not characteristic of him. "I'm sorry."

"We're looking at this thing from opposite sides," she said a little stiffly, "so we're seeing two very different things."

"Have you thought that your refusal to

sell us this right of way might be the means of keeping the Oregon Trunk from being built?"

She stood at the desk, a proud, realistic girl, seeing this exactly as Herb Racine would have seen it, knowing what the consequences of her decision might be, but still holding to that decision. She said: "I have thought about it."

There was no point in continuing the argument. Lee was less interested in the moral issues of the question than he was in the concrete problem of gaining the right to cross her and her neighbors' land without trouble-breeding court proceedings. He had made a significant gain in securing her admission that, of the two evils, she would choose the Oregon Trunk as the lesser. That admission had worried Quinn, and a degree of satisfaction rose in Lee. For the moment both of them were blocked, but given time and the opportunity to use the special talents Stevens had mentioned, Lee Dawes would have the right of way.

Lee nodded cheerfully. "Thanks for the breakfast."

She relaxed, her blue eyes softening. "Willie paid for that."

Picking up his derby, he said good bye and left the house.

Lee found Highpockets doubled over in laughter, Quinn shaking a fist at him, and swearing fiercely. Highpockets straightened up, and wiped his eyes. "You ought to have seen his face, Lee, when he found out them tires was all right."

"Nothing but a sneaking trick to get me out of the house," Quinn said bitterly. "I've got a notion to hit this drink of water so hard his skull will pop out through his head." Then anger went out of Quinn, as Lee had seen happen so many times, and he grinned. "Well, I guess you didn't get anywhere with that lady."

"About as far as you did. I'm glad to see you again, Mike. Been a long time."

Their eyes locked, minds reaching back over their common years, and Quinn nodded. "Ditto, and I guess we'll be seeing each other quite a bit. You're still fast on your feet, son." He motioned toward the car. "I lied about this rig breaking down so she'd put me up all night. Thought I'd talk to her some more today. Didn't figure on you showing up."

"You never know women," Lee taunted. "If you had, you'd have seen last night that she meant no when she said no."

"And you're claiming you know women?"

"I make out."

"Not with a brunette you met on the *Inland Belle*."

"I didn't do so bad. By the way, where is she?"

"That would be none of your business. The claim's staked out, Dawes."

Lee fished for his pipe, wondering at the quick tension that gripped Quinn. "So it's staked out, is it?" he asked.

"You bet it is, and you'd better stick to railroading." Quinn, wheeling, strode into the barn.

Highpockets had already hitched up the livery team. He drove up now, and Lee climbed in. Settling back into the seat, Lee pulled steadily on his pipe while they followed the twin ruts to the road. He thought about the southern lift of the land, and the strategic position this central Oregon plateau held.

"I heard that if they built a railroad through here," he said, "they could start two freight cars from a point south of Bend, give one a push north and the other a push south, and the damned cars would roll clear to Portland and San Francisco."

"Sounds about like some of my yarns." Highpockets chuckled.

Lee scanned the notched skyline of the Cascades running from Bachelor and Broken Top north to Mount Hood and, turning his head, stared at the rugged spread of barren hills stretching away to the east.

"Quite a country, ain't it, son?" Highpockets asked with the pardonable pride of a central Oregonian.

"It is that." Lee pointed his pipe stem toward the mountains. "Talk about Harriman's Fence. Looks like Nature put one up herself."

Highpockets gave him a quick glance. "That's why the Deschutes cañon is so important to your railroad outfits. There are passes through the mountains like the Santiam and McKenzie, but they'd make tough building. Feller named T. Edgenton Hogg had that notion once. Hey, lookit who's coming.

It was cigar-smoking little Cyrus P. Jepson, riding a big black gelding, as neatly dressed as ever, his high-crowned Stetson pointed upward like a diminutive Mount Jefferson. He recognized Lee, and reined up at the edge of the road, his round eyes guarded and thoughtfully fixed on the buggy.

"Want to talk?" Highpockets asked softly.

"If he's got anything to talk about."

Highpockets pulled the team to a stop, and Jepson said with grave courtesy: "Good morning, gentlemen."

"Howdy, Jepson," Lee said. "Quite a way from Jepson City, aren't you?"

"Business held me up. I'm surprised to see you. You missed the stage."

"Had an accident that gave me a bad headache." Watching Jepson closely, Lee could not read the effect of his words upon the little man.

"That's too bad. Well, it's nice to see you again, Dawes. You'll be around Madras for a time?"

Again Lee recognized the deliberate probing. "A few days."

Jepson nodded pleasantly. "I'll see you." Reining his horse around the buggy, he galloped past.

Highpockets spoke to the team, and, as the buggy lurched forward, Lee twisted in the seat, remaining that way until Jepson turned into Hanna's lane. When he shifted back, Highpockets chuckled. "Went in to see Hanna, didn't he?"

"Yeah, and pounding the dirt."

"He got worried when he saw you, and he'll keep sweating until she tells him you ain't bought no right of way through to the Crooked River."

Lee nodded toward the mountains. "How far to the Deschutes?"

"Maybe fifteen miles."

"Think I'll hire a horse. I'd like to see that gut I've been hearing so much about."

"I'll drive you over. Ain't got nothing better to do."

"Not much of a vacation for you, but I'd like it if you want to." After a moment's thought, he added: "You know, it'd clear some things up in my head if I knew for sure Jepson was behind Boston Bull slugging me last night, and if it was Jepson, why."

"You know dad-burned well it was Jepson. You said he was with Hanna on the train. Don't forget she's been away from the ranch. I'd say Jepson tried to make sure you was out of the way till Hanna gave her neighbors a boost." Highpockets paused, one hand coming up to pull thoughtfully at a big ear. "Of course, it might've been that Quinn feller. He could've telephoned to somebody in Shaniko."

"Never thought of that," Lee admitted.

Highpockets sat in silence a moment, his forehead furrowed in thought. "There's one angle I can't figger out. Why's that black-haired Haig filly running with Quinn now? When she first showed up here, she and Jepson was close as two fingers."

"They were?" Lee stared at him in surprise, trying to fit this new fact into the pattern of his puzzle, and failing.

CHAPTER SIX

Lee had dinner in Madras, and, taking a room in the Green Hotel, slept until after darkness had come. He ate supper and afterward strolled idly along the street. Returning to the hotel lobby, he filled his pipe and sat slackly and loosely in the chair, a strange unease riding him. Reaction was setting in from the head-cracking in Shaniko, the fight with Boston Bull, the sleepless night dash, and finally his disappointment at Hanna Racine's.

Highpockets came by, pausing a moment to ask: "What time do you want to go in the morning?"

"Early."

"I'll have the horses here at six." Highpockets nodded, and moved away in the leggy stride of a normal-sized man on stilts.

Lee knocked out his pipe, the smoke bitter and distasteful against his tongue, a sense of the sinister pervading him. This central Oregon was a battleground where men's scheming would presently break into the open, their pressures forcing the pattern of its life into the lower channels of human behavior, exactly as a spring flood would be carried by the cañon passages to the Deschutes. Others would break, but not Hanna Racine. She stood above the greed and the violence, an example of clean, young integrity. He was sure of that, and he wished he could be certain of persuading her to his will.

Lee had breakfast with Highpockets the next morning, and, with the sun pouring its first scarlet tide upon the mountains, they drove north, the cold, crisp air like a tonic. This was another day, and Lee's spirits lifted as the bays moved along the road at their mile-eating clip. They headed toward the great break in the escarpment that Highpockets had pointed out two nights earlier, turned down the deep and narrow gorge of Trout Creek, and on to the vaster rift in the great brown plateau that was the cañon of the Deschutes.

Excitement keening in his blood, Lee stared upward in open-mouthed wonder. Tangible and immediate now were all the things he had tried to visualize to this moment: great cliffs lifting in staggered rises to the blue vault of the spring sky, the tremendous rent that must have come from the tortures to this land that Jepson had mentioned, the cold and turbulent stream hurrying so swiftly to reach the Columbia, the drone of its movement mingling with the myriad echoes along the unending miles.

Highpockets waved a big hand downstream. "Long ways to the Columbia, son. It's just a tunnel with the top off. Only thing is Hill and Harriman didn't dig it. The Lord done that, and I reckon He'll get a chuckle out of their dinky little steam shovels." He motioned toward Trout Creek. "The Harriman survey takes off through there, but the Oregon Trunk goes up the Deschutes to Willow Creek and follows it to the plateau."

The thrill of battle was in Lee again as they rode back to Madras. He could well appreciate now what John Stevens had told him about access to the cañon being one of the major problems of both roads. This would not be a railroad to inch forward in completed sections, as steel is laid in open country. The full length of the cañon would go under construction at once, being marked off into a hundred stations, with an equal number of camps, bringing the entire water level grade into existence simultaneously. Once the cañon walls were notched and chipped away to hold it, the steel would come fast. The fight would be mainly over the right to numerous points of conflict, thousands of men toiling and sweating and cursing to bring the glistening bands first into Madras, on to Bend, and perhaps to California and domination of the West Coast.

It was clear to Lee that at this point the Oregon Trunk had an edge on Harriman's Deschutes Railroad. Under the guidance of W. L. Nelson, the Oregon Trunk had in 1906 located over one hundred miles of railroad through the cañon from the Columbia southward, and had filed its location. From that time until John F. Stevens's acquisition, it had been seeking financing, although its location had roused some question in the Department of the Interior because of a federal power dam envisioned for the Deschutes in the vicinity of Sherars Bridge, and another dam, which was being promoted by private interests, near the mouth of the river.

Stronger than ever in Lee Dawes was the feeling that this thing had exploded into a major railroad battle involving the entire coast. He recalled that in March a representative of Harriman had announced that funds had been set aside to build the Deschutes road and for extension of the Shasta division of the Southern Pacific, currently nearing Klamath Falls, north to meet the Deschutes line at Bend, thus completing a new route from San Francisco to the Columbia. At the same time, Lee had heard talk of the Oregon Trunk's showing interest in a short line owned by a Medford doctor that ran east from that southern Oregon town into the Cascades, with the idea of swinging across the mountains there and heading for California.

Once more it was the life that Lee Dawes loved, and his depression of yesterday was swept away. It was late afternoon when they rode into Madras, a small frontier town set in the bottom of Willow Creek basin.

Highpockets drew up in front of the hotel. "I'll get me a bit of grub and head out, Lee," he said. "Figger I might as well go to The Dalles and see the sights."

Lee, knowing better than to try to pay him for the livery service, held out his hand. "Well, I'll see you, friend. Thanks for everything."

Highpockets grinned and clattered away, and Lee, turning, moved along the street to the hotel.

Mike Quinn's six-passenger Thomas automobile was in front of the hotel. Lee's pulse skipped a beat. Where there was Quinn, there was likely to be Deborah. He went to his room, cleaned up, and was about to leave for supper when, glancing through the window, he saw Quinn throw a suitcase into his automobile, crank it, and drive away.

It was only a hunch, but there was a powerful compulsion in him to act upon it. Descending to the lobby, he asked at the desk: "Has Miss Haig registered yet?"

"Yeah. Room Twenty-Four."

"Thanks." Lee spun and climbed the stairs two at a time.

Number 24 was only two doors from his own. Lee knocked, his heart hammering against his throat, a tightness clinging there. He heard the sound of movement, then the door opened.

"Why, it's Lee Dawes."

Lee went in without invitation. "A little past Shaniko and a little late, but here I am."

Deborah closed the door and stood with her back to it, brown eyes on him questioningly, pleasure mingled with uncertainty in her half smile. "You shouldn't be here, Lee."

"Because of Quinn?"

She looked annoyed. "There is a thing called propriety."

"Has Quinn heard about it?"

She studied him a moment in cool silence.

"There may have been some gossip about us, but I wouldn't take you for a man who would listen to it."

Lee's smile was light and friendly. "That's right. I never listen to gossip. Where was Quinn heading?"

"Horseshoe Bend. I mean . . . well, I'm not sure. Up north. He's all over the country. I probably won't see him for several days."

"Now that's fine." Lee stepped toward her and took her hands. "We might as well make use of those days, since we both have nothing but time on our hands. We'll start by having supper. Seems like I remember having a supper date with you."

The small stiffness left her and she smiled. "You move at a fast pace, Mister Dawes."

"You like it?"

"*Hmm.* Maybe."

"I knew I'd find you again. It had to be that way."

"That sounds a little crazy, as if it was destiny."

"Why not? We're the same kind of people. I want you. You want me. Simple. Why make a problem out of it?"

"It does sound simple," she murmured. Her eyes were pinned on Lee, dark eyes that never lacked the fire of lusty and tempestuous living.

He was suddenly serious now, excitement racing through him with the violence of a heavy wind carrying a crown fire through the timber. "You knew that as well as I did when I kissed you on the boat. You'll never forget that kiss, and neither will I."

"I never will," she said almost breathlessly.

It was, he saw, her subtle way of giving an invitation. "Supper?" he asked.

"Well . . . all right."

Lee hurried to his room, changed to his best clothes, put on bay rum, and combed his hair carefully. The sun had gone down when he left his room again.

Lee, moving hurriedly between his room and Deborah's, saw a man turning down the stairs. He frowned, thinking that from the back it looked like Cyrus P. Jepson. But now his mind was on other things, and he knocked lightly on her door.

Opening it, she asked: "How do you like me?"

She had changed to a white gown that, with the string of pearls at her throat, set off in striking contrast the deep darkness of her hair and eyes, the tanned vitality of her clear skin. Slender and tall, she held her shoulders straight, her lips a strong, scarlet line across her heart-like face.

108

Lee murmured, "And they've never put you on the cover of a magazine."

It was a good meal in the hotel dining room, and there was pride in Lee's eyes as other men turned to look at Deborah. She seemed unduly quiet, yet he sensed that she was finding in this hour the same keen pleasure he was finding.

He had struck fire in her in that long kiss and embrace on the *Inland Belle,* had aroused an urge that would not subside until it had been answered. There had always been a certain detachment in himself, an amused study of the conduct he could inspire. This was new, and he wanted it so, and he wanted her to know that. So he gave her his utmost in gallantry and tenderness, and, when they rose and crossed the dining room, she said: "I'll go up alone."

He looked at her closely, sensing that she did not mean it as dismissal. "All right," he said.

She was standing by the window when he closed the door softly behind him. Turning, she looked at him, the ageless half smile of a woman at destiny's touch breaking on her lips.

"I knew you'd come," she said, and her voice held both regret and exultation. "I'm warning you that I'm bad for you. You'd better pull out before it's too late."

"And I'll be bad for you, so it's a fair trade." He closed the door and stood looking at her, feeling the full depth of the satisfaction this moment held.

"A fair trade," she murmured. "You haven't been able to do business with Hanna Racine, have you? You never will, Lee. She isn't your kind. Why don't you get out of central Oregon, and let people play the game who made the rules?"

He said nothing for a moment, watching her, seeing the sheen of her hair in the lamplight. Drunk as he was with that moment, he didn't understand the full meaning of her words. It was silly, he thought, for her to mention Hanna and business. "I'm the boy who made the first set of rules," he said, and, crossing the worn carpeting, he took her in his arms. Her lips were lifted for his kiss, and he held her hard against him.

Both heard the door open, but, lost in the swirling warmth that enfolded them, Lee paid no attention. It was Deborah who broke away and stepped back swiftly. Lee, turning in the same instant, heard Mike Quinn say: "A pretty picture you make."

Quinn's rugged face wore a smile, but his eyes were deadly cold. Deborah had colored

110

guiltily, but Lee felt only the acute sense of frustration that whetted a razor edge for his temper.

Deborah smiled, and, tossing her head, said: "You never came into my room before without knocking."

"I heard voices. So sweet and low I forgot my manners. My car broke down on this side of Hay Creek." He turned frigid eyes on Lee. "Maybe you'd like to help fix it."

It was the old challenge, just as they had always fought after one of them had been caught poaching on the other. Yet there was a deadly thing between them now that had never been there before. And measuring Quinn, Lee saw something else. Mike Quinn was a man in agony, and it was not like him to feel or look that way about a woman.

"Glad to, Mike," Lee said, and followed Quinn out of the room and into the street.

"We've never decided anything by fighting," Quinn said, "and we can decide this now without it. I'm warning you to stay away from my woman."

"Your woman? That isn't the way she tells it."

"It's the way I tell it. I love her and I've respected her, which is something I know damned well you'd never do." He paused then, his eyes on Lee in the thin light wash-

111

ing through the hotel window, and added, in a voice that was entirely cold: "It's because I love her and because I know what you can do to her that I'm telling you this. Stay away from her, or I'll kill you."

"All right, Mike," Lee said. "That's a little strong, but I feel the same way about Deborah. If you stop me, it'll be the way you threaten."

CHAPTER SEVEN

Quinn and Deborah Haig had checked out of the hotel when Lee came down the next morning, and for a turbulent moment the temptation to follow them was strong in him. But he put down his wild impulse; Stevens had told him to stay here in Madras a few days — and he had no choice.

In the talk on the *Inland Belle,* Stevens had promised detailed instructions regarding the countless right-of-way agreements that Lee would soon be negotiating. Meanwhile, there were two all-important assignments: securing the right of way through Hanna's property, and identifying the mysterious third party Stevens had mentioned.

Lee felt he had made some headway. He was certain he had an edge on Mike Quinn in their dealings with Hanna Racine, and there was little doubt in his mind that Cyrus Jepson either was the third party or was associated with him. Remaining in and around Madras for a week, Lee was surprised at the local support of the people's movement in the northern part of Crook County. Privately he conceded that central Oregon had considerable cause for complaint against the big railroad corporations. It was served now only by the tiny Columbia Southern, and the real wealth of the state's interior lay far south of Shaniko, dependent even now in the twentieth century on stages and freight wagons that belonged to the 1800s. The continually delayed promise of an adequate railroad had become a joke no longer holding humor for these Westerners.

Few thought that either the Oregon Trunk or Harriman's new Deschutes Railroad would actually lay a single rail. "The proposed constitutional amendment is a whiplash to get Harriman to move," a Madras businessman told Lee. "Now, I've got an idea Harriman is kicking up all this smoke just to beat that amendment."

"The Oregon Trunk is something else," Lee said.

The man waved it aside. "Just a two-bit, locally owned outfit aiming to take a bite out of Harriman's pocketbook." He looked at Lee sharply. "Of course, if you're saying the Oregon Trunk is Hill's line, I'd think differently."

"I can't say that," Lee admitted.

"All right." The man smiled sourly. "I guess we'd better have the State of Oregon build some railroad."

It had been announcement piled upon announcement, promise upon promise, and the skepticism of the central Oregon people had grown. Yet Lee was glad to report to Stevens that there was considerable admiration for James J. Hill as a railroad builder, and, if future developments showed that he was behind the Oregon Trunk, public opinion would undoubtedly swing to him in the impending race up the cañon.

Late in April, a development had somewhat crystallized the situation. The *Madras Pioneer* had carried an announcement that Secretary Ballinger of the Interior Department had approved the maps the Harriman people had filed for the first forty miles of their right of way, provided that construction be started immediately. That put it up to the Oregon Trunk. Action would come now, or the whole thing would blow up as it had before.

Lee chose Sunday for another visit to Hanna Racine's place, riding out from Madras on a saddle horse hired from the local livery. It was full spring now, the season's warmth bringing a brightness to the green-floored valleys, a more somber gray-green hue to the sweeping roll of the plateaus. And in the ride Lee found escape from the pressures and irritations that had plagued him almost from the moment he had first seen Deborah Haig coming aboard the *Inland Belle.*

Lee found Hanna in the yard in front of the ranch house, wearing Levi's and spading a flower bed with lithe young energy. Dismounting at the gate, Lee was sure of the pleasure he saw in her eyes.

Smiling, she called: "How are you, Lee?"

"Fine as silk." He moved in quick, long strides to stand beside her. "Got another spade?"

"I guess I could find another one." She looked younger than he had remembered her, almost too young to be a graduate of the University of Oregon, the outdoor air putting a pretty freshness in her face and eyes. "Does it get you, too? This time of year I could swell up and burst."

"Don't do that. It would spoil a mighty pretty arrangement."

She motioned to the Levi's. "I hope this outfit doesn't shock you. I'm one of these modern women, you know. I even refuse to ride a side-saddle."

"I'm shock proof," Lee said lightly.

"Sometimes I go into Bend and play basketball with the girls." She shook her head in mock concern. "I guess we're not considered very proper by the fuddy-duddies. They say we're daring."

"You're just ahead of the times."

She sobered, her eyes on him for a moment before she said: "Yes, I guess that's right."

She was alone, he found, the crew not yet returned from Saturday's towning, and the Indian girl Mary having gone back to Warm Springs for the day. When Hanna saw that he meant to stay a while, she showed him where to put his horse.

Lee carefully avoided mention of the right of way, and Hanna told him about the ranch with enthusiasm kindling in her eyes. Herb Racine had raised cattle and horses in the days when everything between Shaniko Flats and Crooked River was his range, but those days were gone.

"Fences all around us," Hanna said, "and settlers pouring in. What we call progress is coming, and it changes the stock business. The trick now is to breed for quality rather than quantity, and feed to put a little more meat between an animal's hide and bones."

Later in the afternoon, after she had fried a chicken and baked a cake for him, she said: "Thanks for not putting the pressure on me, Lee."

"There doesn't always have to be a railroad between us," Lee said, "although I'll admit I was designing. I'd like to be friends, and I'll promise never to put on the pressure, if you'll make me one promise. Don't close a deal with Mike Quinn without warning me first."

"I can make that promise, because I don't propose to deal with either of you."

He said gravely: "There is one question that's been in my head ever since I saw you on the train with Cyrus Jepson. What do you see in him?"

Hanna laughed. "He's no competition, if that's what you mean. For one thing, he's completely gone on Deborah Haig."

Lee took a sharp breath. "I didn't know that," he said.

Apparently she didn't notice the astonishment in his voice. "I sort of inherited him. He and Dad saw the railroad question alike. Now, he and I see alike. That's all."

They moved across the barnyard to the corral, Lee wondering how a man such as Herb Racine could have been so close to Cyrus Jepson. Unless, and he pondered this, Jepson was entirely different from the way he was visualizing him.

"Highpockets told me your father was killed from ambush. Do you have any idea who did it?" he said.

She regarded him thoughtfully for a moment. Finally she said: "Nothing I could put my hand on. Dad was the kind of man who hewed to the line, and he didn't care where the chips fell. Naturally he made enemies. He particularly hated the kind of promoters who lied in their advertising to attract settlers here. He believed in central Oregon. For years he said it had a big future." She waved a hand northward. "He even dreamed about bringing water from the Deschutes to irrigate a hundred thousand acres of land in this end of the county. Some of the stockmen didn't like to hear that. Then he was the driving force for the people's railroad, in these parts, until he was killed."

Lee's eyes had narrowed. "And Jepson took over that leadership?"

"No, I did. But Jepson has been a good friend and adviser. I don't know how I could have got along without him for a few days after they brought Dad's body in." She shook her head. "I just don't know, Lee, who the murderer was. It must have been some man who hated or feared Dad, perhaps both, and I could name a dozen men who would fill the bill."

As Lee rode back to Madras, he felt he had definitely accomplished something. He could not report success, but he could inform Stevens that the Deschutes Railroad was checkmated on the key Racine property.

It was dusk as he walked from the livery back to the hotel. He saw the big freight outfit pulled up at the edge of the street, but thought nothing about it until he came opposite it, and a man called: "I figgered that was you, Dawes!"

Lee paused, eyes focusing on the big man who stood there beside his team. It was Boston Bull.

Lee stepped toward him, wondering if this was to be another fight. "Want something, Bull?" he asked.

"Yeah, I want something." The big man's knotty face still showed purple and green traces of the free-for-all in the Shaniko saloon. "You ruined me in Shaniko, Dawes. I ain't gonna forget that."

The man's speech was thick and lisping, and Lee remembered the tongue tip that had been sheared off in the fight. Too, there was the pride a man like Boston Bull felt in his fighting prowess, and the licking Lee had given him was a fatal blow to that pride.

"You went out of your way to cook up that fight," Lee said sharply, "and you'd have fixed Highpockets Magoon good if I hadn't taken a hand."

"What we'd have done to Magoon was none of your damned business, mister." Bull spat into the dust. "I'm aiming to collect damages when the sign's right."

"How about right now?" Lee asked softly.

Bull looked along the street, and Lee sensed that the man's brain was fixing on this problem, that he was torn between the hatred he felt for Lee Dawes and the caution that Lee's fists had pounded into him. Revenge, when it came from Boston Bull, would be quick and ruthless, and the middle of a town was no place for it. So he spat again into the dust, and said: "Nope. The sign ain't right. But now you know what's coming. I'm gonna get you, and you're gonna know it before I get you."

"Any time, fella," Lee murmured, and moved on to the hotel.

Lee was due to go on to Bend as Stevens had ordered, and he waited until Highpockets came through with the stage.

"How are you, son?" the tall man called jovially. "Climb up and sit on the throne."

"Thanks."

When they were rolling across the sun-washed land, dust lifting in a smothering cloud from the whirling wheels, Highpockets said: "In case you didn't know, Quinn and that chain-lightning gal of his are in Bend."

"I've wondered."

"And another thing. Jepson's been on one of his three-day toots in Shaniko."

"Jepson's a drinking man?" Lee asked in surprise.

"One of them funny ones. He goes for months and don't touch it. Then he goes on a tear that's a lollapalooza. Stays in his room and sleeps, and, when he wakes up, he takes another snort and passes out again. I sure hate to see a man drink thataway. A crutch is all it is, and it lets a man down in the end."

"Is he still in Shaniko?"

"Nope. Went back to Bend."

"Where did he come from?"

"Frisco. Came in with enough money to jingle loud."

"How did Deborah Haig get tied up with him?"

"Dunno, except that she came from Frisco, too. Some claim she was his woman. Just gossip. I never believed it, but she has done a lot of work for him. You know how a good-looking woman like that can get information out of men who wouldn't talk no other way. And I heard she had some of her own money sunk into that town site of his."

"You think that's straight?"

Highpockets spat into space. "Likely. Everybody's trying to get rich off the other feller, especially the new ones." He grinned. "I'll bet she's taking that Irishman Quinn for a ride that's gonna pinch him before he's done."

They lapsed into silence, Lee filling his pipe and smoking thoughtfully. It made sense that Deborah Haig had a bigger stake in this game than the small spying she would be able to do for Mike Quinn. If she had money invested in the Jepson City town site, the pattern was clearer and far stronger than he had guessed.

The day cooled, and Lee, shivering, drew his coat collar together. He said: "Hell of a spring in this country."

Highpockets chuckled. "Son, don't you know we don't have no spring in this country? Two seasons, winter and August. That's all."

It was Lee's first trip south of Crooked River. They wheeled past rugged Smith Rocks, down the long, steep grade to the river at Trail Crossing, *clattered* across the bridge, and pulled up on the other side.

"Don't look like a railroad ever will cross this cañon," Highpockets said, "but down-river a piece is a spot where the rims are so dad-burned close a grasshopper can spit across. I hear that's where the survey runs." He shot a sideways glance at Lee. "And it's why Hanna's place is the key that unlocks this here whole business."

They rolled into Redmond and beyond, and coming to the Deschutes, crossed it, and presently came to Laidlaw. The road twisted among the junipers and past shacks set in the newly irrigated fields. It was the first time Lee had seen any of the widely advertised irrigation work — private, state-regulated projects coming under the Carey Act — and he realized that only a beginning had been made. They crossed the Deschutes again, still as cold and clear and violent in its hurry to reach the Columbia as it had been where Lee had seen it near the mouth of Trout Creek, wheeled into the picturesque town of Bend, and drew up beside the Pilot Butte Inn, a long, two-story structure set between the road and the river.

Registering, Lee asked for his mail, and went to his room. His mail consisted of a single letter from John Stevens, sharply questioning the delay over the Racine property. There was also a detail map showing the missing parts of the Oregon Trunk right of way — a document, Lee realized, that would be extremely valuable to his opponents.

CHAPTER EIGHT

Lee wrote to Stevens before he went down to supper, a letter that contained more optimism about the Racine property than he actually felt. He mailed it, and went into the dining room for supper. Within a matter of minutes, Cyrus Jepson came in, saw Lee, and sat down at his table.

"How are you?" Jepson asked amiably. "Sometimes I wonder what a railroad finds for its men to do. It seems that I run into a railroad man of one sort or another squatting behind every sagebrush clump."

"That would make a lot of railroad men," Lee said dryly.

Jepson took his cigar out of his mouth, the smoke casting a momentary shadow over his red-cheeked face. "I suppose you're finding plenty to do."

"Plenty." Again Lee felt he was being pumped. He changed the subject. "Coming in on the stage, it struck me this country was about as interesting as that around Biggs."

Jepson fingered the ash from his cigar. "It is. A lava country. Some of the most recent flows in continental United States are within twenty miles of Bend. Of course some of it is very old. For instance, you can find eroded hills up Crooked River that give an idea of what the Paleozoic horizons were. Around Mitchell we can find strata of the age of reptiles. As a matter of fact, the remnants of a pterodactyl have been found. Ever heard of a pterodactyl, Dawes?"

"No." Lee grinned as he reached for the platter of rainbow trout.

"A pterodactyl was a flying dragon, extinct now, of course. At different times, I'd say there were half a dozen seas in central Oregon. On top of the last one we find evidence of the age of mammals. The plant life represented a semi-tropical climate."

"The climate's sure changed," Lee said, thinking how cold he'd been on the seat with Highpockets that day. "In another million years I suppose fellows like you will be talking about the dry, frigid age of sagebrush and junipers."

Jepson leaned forward, round eyes watching Lee's face closely. "The climate *has* changed, and it will change again. It's my opinion it will be very hot for railroad men after November, Nineteen Ten. But to get on with my story. In the strata along the John Day River we have found some very fine fossils of Cenozoic mammals . . . rhinos, oreodons, flesh-tearing cats, and great dogs. Those beds were explored by the famous John Condon. You've heard of him, Dawes?"

"I'm plain ignorant alongside you."

"You're smart, Dawes. Too smart to play errand boy for the Oregon Trunk."

"We settled that in Shaniko, Jepson," Lee said sharply. "Remember?" Reaching again for the trout, he felt the approaching climax of Jepson's talk. The man had not approached him merely to offer another bribe, so Lee kept on eating, lifting his eyes occasionally to Jepson's face.

"Those who adjust themselves to these changes survive. Those who don't . . . die. For example, in this case we had the mid-Miocene mammals such as the three-toed horse and a giraffe camel. Later, there was the ice age. There were interglacial periods, and during one of these we had llamas and many kinds of birds, even the flamingoes."

Jepson paused, half smiling, his gaze steadily on Lee, and Lee, smiling back, felt an edge of disappointment in the man.

"It's amazing, Jepson," Lee murmured, "and some of the people here are as amazing as the geology. For instance, you claim to be a prophet who can foretell the things that will survive and the ones that won't."

"Yes," Jepson said quickly. "I claim to be that much of a prophet, and whether or not you personally survive depends on how well you adjust yourself to the economic changes that are coming in Oregon."

Jepson rose, and Lee said: "Thought you were going to have supper with me."

"No, I've eaten. I just wanted to chat with you. Good night." Jepson nodded, and left the dining room, only the stomach-churning smell of his cigar remaining as a reminder of him.

It was good to have concrete work ahead, and Lee, making the Pilot Butte Inn his base, worked north to Redmond and beyond, filling in the missing pieces of Oregon Trunk right of way. Twice he saw Quinn at a distance, and one morning in Bend he saw Jepson spin past in a buggy, Deborah beside him. Lee called, but Jepson did not look at him; his only response was to lean forward and whip the team to a faster pace. If Deborah saw him, she gave no indication of it, and a sick fear was in Lee that she had not

129

wanted to see him. Standing on a Bond Street corner, Lee watched them take the desert road, and he was remembering that Jepson City lay off somewhere in that direction.

The weeks clipped quickly past. Late in May the town buzzed with the talk that the Oregon Trunk had been given sixty days in which to show it meant business, if approval of its survey maps by the Interior Department was not to be withdrawn. Knowing the mobilizing problems facing both roads, Lee was annoyed by this and the jeering talk it caused. Late in June, Secretary Ballinger abruptly approved the entire surveys of both roads, irrespective of the conflicts between them — leaving the adjustment of such matters to the federal courts.

In a stray copy of the *Madras Pioneer* he found in the hotel, Lee read an account of the railroad story that said that the Harriman line had secured the right of way for seventy percent of the one hundred and twenty miles it proposed to traverse. Lee tipped his hat to Mike Quinn and redoubled his own efforts.

It was on the last Saturday night in June that Lee had a shave and bath in Tripplet's barbershop. When he emerged from the bathroom, he found Mike Quinn waiting his turn.

Quinn raised a hand in salute, and said mockingly: "I suppose the Oregon Trunk has a right of way from here to The Dalles."

"Not quite," Lee said. It was the first time he had talked to Quinn since Quinn had given him the warning in Madras. He waited now, not sure how Quinn would react to his presence.

"Let's get a drink, Lee," Quinn said.

"A drink in this town?" Lee spread his hands in disgust. "Hell, alongside Bend the Sahara Desert is plumb wet."

"It's not that bad. Blind pigs all over the place."

Five minutes later Lee had had his drink. "Looks to me like they might as well open the town as run it this way," he said.

"You know how the Puritans are." Quinn shrugged. "From what I hear the town's half and half."

"What do you mean . . . half and half?"

Quinn grinned. "You can see for yourself, son. Half Bond and half Wall Street."

"Then Bond Street's going to be crowded when the Oregon Trunk gets here. There'll be ten thousand men wanting to drink every Saturday night."

"You think it'll get here?" Quinn lifted a

skeptical brow. "I'd say you were doing more wishing than thinking."

Lee smiled. "We'll see," he said laconically, and left the room.

Early in July the *Bend Bulletin* was popping with railroad news. A man returning to town said that he had seen about a hundred and fifty Italian laborers, and a considerable number of mules, in the vicinity of Grass Valley. He had been told they were to build a wagon road from Grass Valley, on the Columbia Southern, to the river, to provide supplies for the construction crew to come. This piece of concrete action was tonic to the impatient plateau.

Harriman was to seize the strategic points along the line, it was said, without waiting for the conflicts to be decided in the courts. This meant war. Chief Engineer Boschke, of the Harriman lines, equipped and dispatched a record crew of engineers, which reached Grass Valley and left immediately for the Deschutes.

Lee Dawes heard and watched, his own excitement being sharpened by each new piece of news. He was glad to see action breaking into the open at last. It would ease his own labors against the widespread doubt. Too, Grass Valley would be the first hot spot, and, when the action came, it would be fast and perhaps smoky. With that picture prodding his mind, the desire grew in him to be there rather than here in the south.

It was the evening of July 9th that Lee rode into the livery stable, left his horse, and, after a bath at Tripplet's, angled across Wall Street to the Pilot Butte Inn. As he stepped into the lobby, the clerk called — "There's a note here for you, Mister Dawes!" — and slid an envelope across the desk.

Lee tore it open, premonition setting up a faint disturbance along his spine. The note read: *I'm at the Bend Hotel in Room 20. James F. Sampson.*

Lee headed out through the door again, knowing he was in for a hiding from Stevens, who was posing as a man named Sampson, and wanting to get it over with.

John F. Stevens was standing before the window when Lee entered his room in response to the engineer's invitation.

He wheeled around as Lee came in, and his greeting was a sharp question: "Why haven't you got our right of way through the Racine property?"

"If you knew Hanna Racine, you'd know," Lee answered with equal sharpness.

Stevens waved the point aside. "She's a woman, and there are methods for handling every woman. I thought you knew them all."

"I don't know the method for this one," Lee said.

Stevens grunted — "Sit down." — and began pacing the floor, a big man dominated by one compelling urge. Watching him from a chair beside the bed, Lee saw that a change had come over him since their talk on the *Inland Belle*. His temper was honed to a razor sharpness, a tension confirming the fact that things were about to break.

"It's ready to blow, Dawes. Porter Brothers are moving in. Within a few days I'll announce my identity and the fact that Hill is behind the Oregon Trunk." He paced to the window and back. "But that's not the reason I called you over. When we talked on the boat, I told you that the Racine property would be a tough nut to crack." He leveled a finger at Lee. "You're supposed to be an ace trouble-shooter. You don't realize the size of the stack I shoved in behind you, Dawes."

"I'll get it."

"You've got to. The entire success of our tactics depends on you getting that right of way. We can't keep stalling around. We can start condemnation proceedings. . . ."

"I wouldn't advise that, sir," Lee cut in.

"Oh, you wouldn't advise it. And why?"

"Because Hanna will fight it, and her neighbors will fight it, and we'll kick up a hell of a lot of bitterness. With this people's movement going on the ballot, we need all the public support we can get. This road will be here a long time, Mister Stevens. It strikes me that good will is worth waiting for."

Stevens stood pulling at his mustache, a half smile striking at the corners of his mouth. "There's some horse sense in what you're saying, all right."

"Time is on our side. If we let the people's movement run under its own power, it'll bust itself. One of these days Hanna will do business with me in her own way and her own time."

Stevens nodded, the anger gone out of him. "All right, Dawes. Now about the second assignment I gave you."

Lee pulled his pipe from his pocket and dribbled tobacco into the bowl. "I've done a little better on that. I'm sure it's the people's movement, and our third party is Cyrus P. Jepson, but so far I've got no proof, nor any evidence that he's done anything criminal."

Lee told what had happened, and, when

135

he was done, Stevens nodded. "I remember Jepson City. Nothing unusual about it." He thought about it a moment, and then asked skeptically: "It would seem, the way you tell it, that Jepson is using the people's movement for his own selfish purpose. Why?"

"I think I've figured out the answer. There are no towns between Bend and Burns. Jepson undoubtedly feels that the proposed people's east-west railroad will go through his town site. If that country becomes a wheat-growing section, as people think it will, there will be a good-size town somewhere out there in the desert. If Jepson City happens to be that town, Jepson stands to make a million dollars."

Stevens nodded. "That might be the story. Well, Dawes, keep your eye on this Jepson. If you've got it sized up right, he'll come into the open with some definite action. Then do what you have to do. And about Hanna Racine. It's something new for me to have my railroad hanging on a woman's whim. Wind it up as soon as you can, because I want you in Grass Valley."

A quick, expectant grin broke across Lee's tanned face. "I was hoping to hear that."

"There's a stretch below Sherars Bridge called Horseshoe Bend, with room for only one good roadbed through it. The Harriman people got the jump on us by putting in a big camp and building an access road. I wish we could throw a monkey wrench into their machinery, but I don't see how. In any case, you'll report to Porter Brothers, and be on hand if they need a man of your caliber. I'm guessing that Jepson will be around Shaniko or Grass Valley when the music starts. And" — Lee had paused at the door — "I'll expect you to have the Racine right-of-way agreement in your pocket."

CHAPTER NINE

Summer had come to central Oregon, with some of the days cloudlessly bright and warm, the nights cool and softly starred, or again with thunderheads rising, black and grim, on the Cascade skyline. At times storms struck in the mountains or foothills or in the eastward desert, sharply and without warning, with ragged flashes of lightning running through a close bombardment of thunder.

Sometimes nearly half an inch of precipitation fell in an afternoon, first hail, and then rain, with pools forming in the ruts of Wall and Bond Streets in Bend, water stirring their surfaces with constant unease and streaming from roofs in swift, noisy streams. Always, then, the air, so high and thin and crystalline, became pungent with the heady tang of sage that was like wine taken in great drafts.

Searching the town one Saturday afternoon for a farmer with whom he had been unable to deal, Lee was caught by the rain in front of Lara's store. He stepped inside, bought some fishing tackle, and, seeing Hanna at the dry-goods counter, crossed to her. He said: "So you've come to taste the excitement of city life."

Hanna whirled, recognized him, and smiled. "It's just lucky for you I wasn't carrying my gun. I shoot men who come up behind me and scare me."

"I hope you're staying in town," he said. "I owe you a meal or two."

She nodded guardedly. "It's a long way back to the ranch."

"Then let's have supper at the inn. They keep trout on the table every day, and that's something I never had enough of in my life until I came to Bend." He showed her the flies he had bought. "I'm learning to fish, but when I catch one, it's because of something I accidentally do right. Now . . . about supper?"

She hesitated a moment, and Lee, watching her, sensed that she was thinking about the time on the *Inland Belle* when he'd left her standing beside the rail and had gone to search for Deborah Haig. Then she smiled, as if putting it out of her mind, and said: "Why yes, if you like."

"Where are you staying?"

"At the Bend Hotel."

"I'll meet you in the lobby at six." He lifted his hat, nodded, and left the store.

Lee was surprised how much his running into her had lifted his spirits. Five o'clock found him in his room putting on his best suit, and he was waiting in the lobby fifteen minutes before the hour. When she came down the stairs, she looked at him, noting his careful grooming, and said ruefully: "No fair. I didn't come to town prepared to make myself beautiful."

They sat beside an open window in the dining room. Sunlight laced by the shadows of pine needles fell on Hanna's hair, painting a golden glow upon her head. Lee, watching her and seeing the keenness of the quick expressions that crossed her face, felt a rising admiration for this girl, so alive and utterly honest. And for this hour she was the focal point of all his interests.

"Always the rainbows," Lee murmured, and passed the platter of trout to her.

"I wish I could make up my mind about you," Hanna said.

"I'm no puzzle," he said quickly.

She lifted a trout to her plate. "You are to me. Perhaps it's because we live in different worlds. Highpockets was talking about you the other day, and he thinks you're the biggest man who ever walked."

He looked at her in sharp surprise. "Thanks. I'll tell you something nice someday."

"You're a man's man. And a woman's man in a way that sort of scares me. Life seems to be a series of rooms to you. You have such a good time in each one, and then rush madly into the next one."

"I hadn't thought of it that way."

"Lee, you're missing a great deal in not having a room of your own, a room that echoes your yesterdays, and all your tomorrows."

He shook his head, dry amusement curving his lips in a smile. Again this sharp-minded, pretty girl was talking in a way he had never heard a woman talk. "I'm afraid I'd feel cooped up in that room."

Hanna smiled. "Have some more trout, Mister Dawes. I guess you'll spend your life rushing through other men's rooms."

When they had eaten, he said: "Let's have a look at the river."

She nodded her agreement, and, circling the inn, they found a place among the pines on the riverbank. Lee filled his pipe, finding the tension that had gripped him since Stevens's visit completely gone.

"What will you do when this is over?" Hanna asked suddenly.

"Hadn't thought about it." He wondered why she took such pleasure in dissecting him. "I guess there'll always be railroads to build. Mexico. Maybe China."

"The Mexican *señoritas* would appeal to you," she said lightly.

He chuckled as he thumbed tobacco tightly into his pipe. "They're a tempestuous lot. Quinn and I were together in Nicaragua."

"Was that where you knew him?"

"It goes back further than that." He lighted his pipe, and said between puffs: "I'm not trying to start another argument, but my boss mentioned forcing a right of way through your property. I talked him out of it for the moment."

"I'm sorry, Lee," she said flatly. "I made a sort of promise to my father when they brought his body in from the Trail Crossing bridge."

"I respect him and you, Hanna, but I can't see why it should be a matter of principle."

She placed her hands, palm down, on the needled ground behind her and leaned back, eyes on the Cascades, where snow peaks flamed in the dying light of the sun. "It's something you feel, Lee, a kind of

142

workaday religion. This state has taken such a kicking around from big railroad interests. Your Jim Hill once asked . . . 'What must we do to be fed?' Have you ever thought about the countless people who have come here trying to answer that question? I have, Lee, because I've seen them. Everything they owned in a covered wagon that was held together by rope and bailing wire. Sometimes they've starved and moved on, but lots of them make a living, which means they've lived through the vastness and silence and terror of the desert trying to answer Hill's question. Hill doesn't give them any answer . . . not to my little people. And the Harriman Fence has kept out other railroads. That's why Jepson says the Lord gave us a bright land, but there are man-made shadows upon it."

"The Oregon Trunk is breaking down that fence, Hanna."

Her eyes were on him gravely. "What will it be after you've broken it down?"

He was getting nowhere, and he saw that emotions had set her attitudes strongly. He said: "If we condemn through your property, you've lost."

"Losing and giving up are two different things, Lee. There will be so many opportunities for a man like you here. Why

143

don't you stay?"

"I'm afraid Horace Greeley's advice was not aimed at me."

"But this is the last frontier, Lee."

He shook his head. "No. There'll always be a frontier. Somewhere. There are a lot of hills to climb."

"So you can see on the other side. So many things yet for you to do, a lot of women to love, a lot of liquor to drink, and a lot of fights with Mike Quinn."

"I guess that's right."

"Not what I'd call a frontier."

Suddenly he was irritated. It seemed to him that she was like a little boy who had stumbled upon a new clock, and was bound to take it apart to see what made it run. Then she was equally determined to put it back together again and gear it to operate at a different speed and in a different direction. He said with more sharpness than he intended: "Someday you'll forget yourself, and have a good time."

She rose, and stood looking down at him, slim and small and shapely. And desirable. "Perhaps someday I will," she said softly, and, whirling, walked rapidly away.

Lee caught up with her, knowing he had made another mistake. Lee Dawes, expert with women, had been given this job because a woman held a crucial position, and he had fumbled it again because he knew nothing at all about Hanna Racine. He walked in silence beside her to the Bend Hotel, reaching into his mind for something to restore that spirit of warm understanding that he had thoughtlessly destroyed.

He stood in front of the hotel, facing her, and said more humbly than was his habit: "I've got a cousin who's a bull. Once he got into a china shop."

She smiled. "I heard about that cousin."

"Maybe I'll change someday."

"And maybe someday I'll forget myself." She stood with the light from the hotel lobby cutting directly across her face, and Lee saw that her cheeks were bright with color. Then she shook her head, sobering. "I don't think people ever really change, Lee," she said. "Good night."

Lee left Bend the next day, spent some time in Madras buying right of way in the Agency Plains, then took the stage north to Shaniko when he received a letter from Stevens instructing him to get in touch with Johnson Porter at Grass Valley.

He had watched the newspapers for railroad news, and the pattern was shaping rapidly. Twohy Brothers was to build for

Harriman's Deschutes Railroad. Six office rooms had been rented and field headquarters established in the town. A warehouse had been secured for a commissary, and was rapidly being filled with supplies for men and horses. And a large cellar for storing blasting powder had been built.

Lee grinned when he read an editorial in the *Madras Pioneer* inspired by this sudden mobilization of Harriman forces. The *Pioneer* offered an opinion that the Oregon Trunk now appeared to be a dead project, and Lee wondered what the editor would think when the Hill forces drew up, as they would now any day.

Reaching Shaniko, Lee saw in graphic swiftness what the railroads would do to central Oregon. He got the last room in the Columbia Southern Hotel; he had to wait in line for a chair in the dining room. Later in the evening he found the saloons so packed that he had to reach over a man's shoulder to lift his drink from the bar. He cruised along the sidewalk, noting the campfires around the town, the distant and plaintive cry of a baby, the shrill and nagging tone of a woman scolding her husband.

They were all here: freighters, railroad laborers and camp followers, sheepmen, cowboys, land locators and hungry-eyed, pinched-faced farming families from Iowa, Illinois, the Dakotas, Minnesota, seeking their own land, bound for the high desert east of Bend or the Fort Rock and Silver Lake country farther east and south. This was the last big chance for free homes, three hundred and twenty acres that the government said was wheat land. It was to be their own — to till and work, to fence and build upon. They were here to claim that heritage that had been an American farmer's from the early days of settlement.

Their land, Lee thought as he saw them talking in knots along the crowded streets, theirs to dream about and starve upon. Conscience stirred in him momentarily, for many of these people would not be here if the railroad companies had not advertised this homestead country and offered colonists' rates. Then he shrugged and went back to his hotel room, thinking that for an instant he had seen it from the eyes of Hanna Racine and wondering at this.

Lee got out the map Stevens had sent him and studied the lower end of the Deschutes cañon. It twisted northward to the Columbia, not more than five or six miles from Grass Valley, which was thirty miles or so below Shaniko. Harriman's Deschutes Railroad was located on the east side of the river, the Oregon Trunk on the west. The Harriman people would get their supplies from points like Moro and Grass Valley on the Columbia Southern without having to ferry the Deschutes, and their problem of transportation would be far simpler than Porter Brothers'.

It was while brooding over this advantage to the Harriman construction outfits that an idea began churning in Lee's mind, and the more he studied the situation, the more excited he became. The newspapers had reported that Twohy Brothers had gathered men and equipment to build a wagon road from Grass Valley into the cañon. It was generally believed that the Harriman men had decided to seize the strategic points without waiting for the courts to decide the conflicts at such locations.

Lying west of the little town of Grass Valley, Horseshoe Bend was such a point, a long, looping curve providing only one good roadbed. Already Lee had heard enough to believe that a Harriman camp was being established there with the hope of applying the principle of first construction and use it in the court struggle over the site. He remembered Stevens mentioning that an Oregon Trunk camp would be there, too, and Deborah had made a slip-tongue re-

148

mark about Quinn heading this way, the night he had interrupted a nice little interlude. Lee folded the map, knowing that his idea was either a stroke of genius or nothing at all, depending on whether the Harriman people had carefully nailed down all the loose ends.

The train deposited Lee in Moro at 9:10 the following morning. He went directly to the clerk in the Sherman County Courthouse atop the hill. Half an hour later he hired a livery rig and returned to Grass Valley, elation running a swift stream through him. What he was doing would either offset his lack of progress with Hanna Racine or cost him his job.

He had noted it briefly as the train passed through earlier that morning, but aground now in Grass Valley he was astonished at the change that had come over the sleepy little town. Mainly it was the influx of people, but the freight yards were tightly crammed with flats and gondolas and boxcars packed tightly with construction equipment and materials, outfitting for the tremendous camps to be established and food supplies for men and animals. All along the fringes of the town, knocked-down wagons were being assembled to go into the staggering haul; horse teams and pack mules churned the dust into a choking haze. Still on the cars and scattered far and wide on vacant lots and in the fields were scrapers, work cars, lumber, camp ranges, tenting, steel, drilling machinery, and tremendous heaps of commissary stores.

Lee spent some time making inquiries in Grass Valley, called at the French and Downing store, and hired another rig to take him into the country between Grass Valley and the cañon. Here, too, there was a tremendous change. Hordes of workers, largely Italians, having come to Grass Valley on the train and finding no means of transportation, were moving on foot to the first construction camps. Dust boiled everywhere along the way from freshly cut roads, rising behind four- and six-horse freight wagons, behind hacks and buggies and occasional automobiles.

It was mid-afternoon before Lee returned to town. He went directly to Porter Brothers' office. He was told that Johnson Porter was busy with a reporter, and was asked to wait. When the reporter left, a tall man came to the doorway of the inner office. He looked at Lee, and asked: "Were you waiting to see me?" Then a smile broke across his face. "Why, how are you, Dawes?"

"How are you, Mister Porter?" Lee shook

150

the tall man's hand and, when Porter stepped inside, went on into the office. There he stopped in surprise. John Stevens was sitting in the corner, a broad grin on his face.

"Glad to see you, Dawes," Stevens said, and waved toward a chair.

Porter had closed the door behind Lee. Now he asked: "How's our miracle man?"

"Out of miracles right now," Lee answered dryly, "but I have a proposition to make."

"A red herring to make us forget a certain Hanna Racine," Stevens murmured. "Go ahead."

"We're a long way from laying steel across Hanna Racine's place," Lee said, excitement running high in him. The next few minutes would make or break him with John Stevens. "It strikes me that our problem with Hanna will not press us for several months, but there is a ten thousand dollar wagon road the Twohys built that's important right now. You said once, Mister Stevens, we'd have a camp at Horseshoe Bend. I was wondering how you were planning to get supplies to that camp?"

Stevens and Porter exchanged glances. Then Stevens said soberly: "That's a question we haven't answered."

"I suggest we use the road the Twohys built."

"They'd like that," Stevens snorted. "A practical suggestion, Dawes."

"I think it is." Lee grinned. "You see, the Twohys forgot to nail down everything." He saw that he had aroused quick interest in both men, and he went on: "They got permission from the owners of the land to build their roads, and apparently they figured that was enough, but they failed to take deeds to a roadway or to sign an agreement as to the use of the land. The titles were still in the names of Fred Girt, French and Downing, and Roy J. Baker. Why don't we buy their places?"

There was a breathless moment while Stevens and Porter thought about this suggestion. Then Johnson Porter said softly: "Why don't we?"

"We can't close off their road forever," Lee went on, "and we'll get some heads cracked. We'll probably wind up in court, but I'll guarantee one thing . . . the Twohys won't be building Mister Harriman's road as fast as they'd planned."

"What if the owners won't sell?" Stevens asked.

"They will." Lee drew some papers from his coat pocket and handed them to Stevens.

"I've already closed the deal."

Stevens stared at Lee in wide-eyed amazement. He looked at Porter, who had started to laugh, and back at Lee. Then he got up and walked across the room. Suddenly Stevens began to laugh, the loudest and longest laugh Lee had ever heard come from him. He wiped his eyes, and winked at Porter. "Maybe we have got a miracle man, Johnson. I was afraid he'd lost his touch." He nodded at Lee. "I guess this buys you a little more time with the Racine girl."

"I think a little time is the answer, Mister Stevens."

"I hope you didn't bankrupt us buying those ranches."

"These are contracts of sale, and the price was reasonable." Lee smiled. "Later we can complete the purchase, or let them go back. Now I'll get over to Moro and file them with the county clerk."

Johnson Porter was still laughing. "I'd like to see Judge Twohy's face when he hears about this. Nobody ever gets as mad as the judge. Nobody ever gets as mad as an Irishman, anyhow, and Judge Twohy is all Irish." He looked at Stevens. "How about letting me keep this man? There'll be plenty of spots where I can use him."

"You can have him," Stevens agreed, "as

long as he can keep working on the two assignments I gave him. I may have other chores later, but right now he'd better handle this hornet's nest he just kicked over." He was sober now, eyes pinned on Lee. "You'll have hornets buzzing in all directions, son."

"I'll duck 'em." Lee's grin was a quick break across his lean face. He swung to face Porter. "I'll need a few men. We'll get a couple of gates across Mister Harriman's ten-thousand-dollar road, and I'll want padlocks. Big ones."

"You'll get them," Johnson Porter promised.

"One more thing." Lee swung back to face Stevens. "I'd like to put a man named Highpockets Magoon on the payroll. He's done me a lot of good already, and he knows everybody from Shaniko to Bend. Besides, he's an old friend of Hanna Racine."

"Write your own ticket, Lee." Stevens glanced at his watch. "I've got to get back to The Dalles. You'd better tend to filing those sales contracts, Johnson, and let Lee get out on the job." The line head grinned, an eye closing momentarily in a wink. "And, Lee, don't play too rough."

CHAPTER TEN

If Nature could have foreseen the clash of brains and brawn that soon was to grip the attention of all of Oregon and the railroad world, she could not have better prepared the Girt homestead for the purpose Lee intended using it. It lay on the plateau at the very rim of the vast and awesome Deschutes cañon, which dropped two thousand feet to the river. Here two smaller lateral cañons angled nearly together on either side of the great bluff down which Twohy Brothers' new road twisted in a two mile, twenty percent grade to water level, so narrow that only in three places could wagons pass. There was no route by which a wagon road could connect the rail point of Grass Valley with this road except by crossing the Girt homestead, which set athwart the apex of the angle formed by the cañons, in stubborn perversity.

Horseshoe Bend was a huge curve in the

Deschutes, one and a half miles around, a tongue of land running the length of the curve that was one thousand feet across at the base. The natural approach to the engineering problem at this point was a tunnel across the base, by which some eight thousand feet of difficult rock excavation could be avoided — and there was room for only one.

Twohy Brothers had reached the site first, and had established camps on the brink of the bluff. It had taken two hundred men twenty days to build the access road, and, when it was finished, the camps on the bluff had been moved into the cañon. Three hundred men now were preparing to begin work on either end of the tunnel. With the seizure of the Girt homestead they were cut off from equipment, materials, and supplies.

It was dark when Lee reached the Girt place with Johnson Porter, who had decided to come with him, and a handful of men. They could hear the dim growl of the river, and stars made a sharp brightness across the sky. They swung to the ground, and stretched their legs.

Quickly Lee put his crew to work. They found the Girt homestead fenced with barbed wire, the road entering the upper side of the place through a wire gate and leaving by a board gate just before it tipped into the cañon. The men pitched a tent fifty feet from the wire gate, left supplies and two Winchesters, then chained and padlocked both gates.

There was no retreating now, and Lee, watching Johnson Porter as they stood beside a fire the men had built, sensed that the tall man was aware of that fact.

"Just one point in twenty-nine miles of the cañon that's in conflict," Porter said, and chuckled softly. "We have prior claim, but it won't be so good if the Twohys get in first construction. You've eased a big worry for me, Lee. They'll be ready to start digging their tunnel right away, while we're only now getting our heavy equipment into The Dalles, and there's a lot of rough country to cross. Now we can establish our own camp down there at once, and we'll have a road to haul our stuff over."

Filling his pipe, Lee nodded. "They can get some food and horse feed down by pack train, using Max or Sixteen Cañon, but they'll have a tough time getting heavy stuff like scrapers and work cars down on pack mules." He brought a match to life and sucked the flame into the bowl. "One thing worries me. I know Mike Quinn. He's got a way of coming up with a Sunday punch when you aren't looking."

"Then it's up to you to keep looking," Porter said dryly.

There was silence for a time, the men smoking and staring into the fire, the possible results of this step weighing heavily on all of them, for two miles below were three hundred men who would react to this move in characteristic railroad-building fashion, while what would happen in the Harriman field quarters at Grass Valley and again in Portland was beyond reckoning.

Before dawn they cooked a meal, and, when they had eaten, Porter said: "Guess it's time to roll. Lee, I'll get word to Magoon in Shaniko. I'll leave Baldy" — he nodded at a square-built man who stood across the fire from Lee — "with you. The fewer men you have on hand, the less likely you are to touch off violence. Have you got a revolver?"

Lee nodded. "Took it out of my grip before I left Grass Valley."

"Keep it in your pocket. There'll be reporters around, and there's no sense in getting any more adverse publicity than we can help." He stood kicking at the fire, a tall, almost gaunt man, lean face red in the light of the flames. "No Twohy freight wagons go through. Beyond that you're free

158

to use your own judgment. We'll stand on our legal rights. If there's any show of force, let it come from them."

"Baldy says the Harriman camps have been getting their water from some springs up on top. How about that?"

"If it's on our property, we'll use the water." He pinned his eyes on Lee for a moment, then wheeled away from the fire. He said: "Let's roll."

A moment later they had disappeared into the darkness, the clatter of wheels dying in the distance. Filling his pipe again and lighting it, Lee took a moment to study Baldy, a middle-aged, mustached man with kindly gray eyes and the seamy, weather-beaten face of one who belongs under the sun, his feet in stubble or the furrow of a plowed grain field. Whether he had the sand in his craw to stand up under what lay ahead Lee couldn't tell, but he was certain that the man was thoroughly honest and level-headed.

"Let's turn off their water, Baldy," Lee said presently. He had brought a number of *No Trespass* signs. He got one from the tent, and fishing a stubby pencil from his pocket, printed in high letters: *NO WATER TO SPARE. PORTER BROTHERS.* He handed it to Baldy with a grin. "Go get us a bucket of water and tack that up by the spring."

With a hammer, tacks, and a bundle of trespass warnings, Lee set to work. Moving first south and then north, he spaced the signs at regular intervals, tacking them firmly to the juniper posts, so that no wind could blow them off. He saved one for the lower gate, and, when he had finished, the gray half light of dawn had spread across the land.

The air was thin and cold and Lee shivered a little as he turned toward camp. The dusty smell of the hoof-churned earth was in the air; the faint sound of Baldy's throaty cough came to him. Then Lee was pitching forward in a reflex movement. It had come without warning, the *thwack* of a bullet cutting through the crown of his hat, the sharp report of a Winchester breaking into the lonely quiet.

Lee, acting involuntarily, rolled over and jerked the gun from his pocket. There was no cover within fifty yards. He lay, nerves taut, cocked gun held in front of him, eyes searching the rim of the side cañon and expecting a bullet that never came. Presently he heard the run of a horse, and he caught the blur of the animal as it came onto the plateau from the side cañon, the rider bending low in the saddle. A moment

160

later horse and man disappeared.

Baldy came running from the camp, a Winchester in his hand. He called: "Still on your feet, Dawes?"

"I managed to climb back on them," Lee answered with more coolness than he felt. He took off his Stetson, and poked a finger through the bullet hole. "He wasn't fooling, whoever he was."

Baldy swore fiercely. "How'd they guess what we was up to?"

"Somebody's watching every move we make," Lee said somberly, "and they've got damned good eyes."

They turned back toward camp, Lee thinking about this attack. The man had been waiting for him, had fired from deliberate ambush. It didn't square with Harriman tactics nor with Mike Quinn. His thoughts ran swiftly back to his talks with John Stevens, and the mysterious third party. The man who had slugged him behind the Shaniko hotel would be capable of this kind of attack. It could well be Boston Bull, with Cyrus P. Jepson the driving power behind the attempted killing. But why? Lee could find no answer, except the personal hatred Bull felt for him, and that could hardly account for an attack at this particular place and time.

161

The sun was up by the time they reached the tent, crimson streamers flowing across the land, the eastern hills dark purple with receding shadows.

"I'll tack this other sign up at the lower gate," Lee said, and swung away along the road.

It was at the lower gate that Lee got his second look into the great cañon. The river ran like a looping silver cord far below. He could see the Harriman camp, the tents, like dirty gray handkerchiefs, spread on the riverbank. Men moving toward what was apparently the newly started portals of the tunnel were like tiny stick figures.

He could see the looping tongue that made Horseshoe Bend. Beyond the river, a precipice lifted in a half circle for three thousand feet, sheer rock that ledged back only slightly as it rose. No road would ever be built down that wall. This, then, was the one access to Horseshoe Bend.

A sudden chill raveled along his spine as he thought of his part in this, and he thrilled to the thought, satisfaction a pleasant warmth in him. He smiled as he caught a little of the feeling that would be in the Two-hys and Mike Quinn when they learned of this shift in the fortunes of war, and he sensed the big events that would be built upon this cool, breeze-swept dawn.

Lee tacked his remaining trespass warning to the top board of the gate, and returned to camp. Baldy had built up the fire, and the smell of frying bacon rode the air, and hurried Lee's step.

"Our fun will start before long," Lee said as he came up to the fire. "About noon maybe."

Looking up from where he squatted beside the coffee pot, Baldy fixed his eyes on the bullet hole in Lee's hat. He said solemnly: "Damn it, Dawes, I plumb forgot to fix my will before I left town."

Lee's guess proved close to right. Shortly after noon, Mike Quinn and a man with a sheriff's star on his chest rode up to the gate. Seeing them coming, Lee said: "Baldy, stay inside the tent with a Winchester handy. I don't look for trouble, but I like to have some backing."

Moving to the wire gate, Lee stood there, a small grin on his lips.

Quinn reined his horse to a stop, and stood glaring down at Lee for a long and pregnant moment.

"Going fishing, Mike?" Lee asked. "Kind of late in the season. You'd better go back and try it again about next spring. The railroad will be built then."

Quinn swung down and strode forward, powerful shoulders rolled into a menacing hunch. He poked a stubby finger at the *No Trespass* sign. "Throw the damned sign away and unlock the gate. We built this road, and we figure to use it."

"Your road's right where you left it, Mike," Lee said easily. "It's on government land, and we've sure got no objection to your using it, but this is private land belonging to Porter Brothers. They don't want it all messed up with wheel tracks."

Quinn scowled, fingertips massaging a blocky chin. He said: "Dawes, I doubt that you ever bought this land."

"He'd better have," the sheriff said darkly.

Lee drew a folded paper from his pocket. "Got some doubt, have you, Mike? Then listen to this contract of sale. It says . . . 'Fred Girt to Johnson Porter. This agreement made and entered into the Twenty-Fifth day of July, Nineteen Oh Nine, by and between Fred Girt of Sherman county . . .' "

"We haven't got time to listen to no damned legal document," Quinn growled.

"I'm just aiming to settle your doubts." Lee's tone was gently prodding. "I'll skip on down to where it says . . . 'It is further mutually agreed that possession shall be given to grantees at the signing of this

164

contract.' " Lee raised his eyes to Quinn. "Porter Brothers has taken possession, Mike."

"We were tipped off by a man in a position to know, Dawes, but I wanted to see if you were fool enough to think you could pull this off. We can condemn a road across this place."

"And by that time we'll be halfway to Trout Creek."

Quinn wheeled to face the sheriff. "I've got some wagons in Grass Valley loaded with supplies for the camps. What are you going to do about this?"

"Seeing as they locked the gate and posted the land, I don't know what I can do, Quinn. They're inside the law. After hearing that contract, I don't have any doubts about their rights."

Quinn cuffed back his hat, anger bringing its color all the way to his sandy hair, the twist of his lips showing the bitter taste of frustration. Without a word he stepped back into the saddle, wheeled his horse, and galloped back toward Grass Valley, the sheriff beside him.

Baldy came out of the tent. "What do you make of it?"

"We'll hear from that Irishman again," Lee answered.

Late in the afternoon an automobile came grinding over the rough road, a long plume of dust trailing it, swung around at the gate, and a man stepped down. "I'd like to get through!" he called.

Watching from the second post, Lee guessed he was a reporter. "You a Twohy man?"

"No. I want to find out what they're thinking of this in camp."

"Where you from?"

"Portland."

"All right," Lee said. "You can go through if you want to walk."

"Thanks." The reporter paid the driver, and crawled under the barbed wire. He stood eyeing Lee a moment. "You aren't armed, are you?"

"See a gun?"

"That side pocket has a suspicious bulge."

"Full of crackers. I feed 'em to the sidehill gougers. Ever see a sidehill gouger, mister?"

"No."

"Keep your eyes open when you go down the road. You might stumble on one. Front and hind legs on their left sides are 'bout six inches shorter'n the right ones, so they can only travel on the side of the cañon. Can't turn around. Just got to keep going." Lee shook his head. "I feel sorry for the little devils. Fact is, they're damned near extinct."

The man grinned politely, and walked on toward the cañon.

The hours wore on to evening, and no one came from the Harriman camps in the cañon or from town. Returning from the spring with a bucket of water, Baldy said: "There's a bunch of our wagons headed here from The Dalles. Some of 'em oughta pull in tonight."

Lee nodded. "We're really going to kick this hornet's nest over when we set up a camp below here. Baldy, did you ever do any blasting?"

"Some."

"If you're game to take a swing down the road, it might be a good idea to take a look before we put our wagons over it."

Baldy stared. "You think they've got some powder holes in that road?"

"It'd be a damned poor thing to find out with our outfit halfway down."

Baldy picked up a Winchester and set a fast pace toward the lower gate.

The sun dropped over the Cascades and shadows came into the great cañon, forming a strange, purple dusk. Darkness followed, soundless and still, and a cold came to the air and night was all about, hiding the movements and purposes of men. Then a pulse quickened in Lee. Wagons were rolling in from the plateau, and presently their shadows bulked darkly across the fence. Lee drew a gun, and waited until a man called: "This is a Porter wagon train, guard! Open up!"

"Let's have a look," Lee answered, the cock of his gun an ominous punctuation to his words.

Men loomed in the darkness. One struck a match, holding it to his face and that of the man beside him, and Lee saw they were men who had been with him the night before. He unlocked and swung back the gate. The wagons rolled through, heavy and dusty, horses and men lax with travel weariness. A stooped man with glasses, who seemed to be the wagon master, stood at the fire until the gates were closed and locked. When Lee came up to him, he said: "We'll go down tonight."

Lee stared incredulously. "You're crazy. That isn't a road. It's a goat trail."

"The boss said we had to get to digging a tunnel in the morning."

"How many men have you got?"

"Thirty."

"Thirty, and you want to go down there and get chummy with three hundred Harriman men? Mister, they'll throw you into the Deschutes, and first thing you know you'll be in the Columbia."

Baldy emerged from the darkness and came to the fire. He nodded to the wagon master. "Howdy, Sam. Better unhitch and cook your supper."

"We're going on down."

Baldy's glance switched to Lee, his lips holding a thin smile. "Then you'd better fix yourself with the Almighty before you start, because there's enough powder under that road to blow it to the sky in one piece. In the dark it'll be a cinch for them to sneak men up to light the fuses."

The stooped man shrugged. "Hell, they won't touch it off till they know they ain't getting it back. We're rolling down."

"I guess I'll go along," Lee said. "I'm supposed to be running this part of the show, and, if that's where the fun's going to be, I'll mosey on down with you boys and see it."

CHAPTER ELEVEN

They came down the road like stars wheeling across the sky. Brakes locked, lanterns swinging, they came with dust boiling behind them and rocks rolling down the face of the cliff and bouncing into dizzy space and falling like mammoth hailstones into the Harriman camp. They came with strong arms holding to lines, a stream of oaths pouring upon the horses, comforting and guiding them as only teamsters' oaths can, down the switchbacks along a twenty percent grade, around twists in the narrow road, with open space hanging below. And above all of it was the shadowing knowledge that they were traveling over live powder that might at any moment send them pinwheeling into eternity.

Below the road the Harriman camp stirred into action. Lights sprang to life. Men called and hurried from tents to stare upward. One shouted: "There's a million of them!"

"There's only a handful!" the engineer yelled. "They won't do anything except start digging so they can tie us up in the courts."

An American pushed his way through the crowd of Italian laborers. "Want us to set 'em off, boss?" he asked.

"No. There aren't enough to hurt us. Marstoni, get your men dressed and start 'em to shoveling. If they take us into court, we'll show them we meant to dig a tunnel."

But the Hill men did not have their minds on tunnel digging that night. They rolled onto the flat beside the river, the stooped man stepping down and with a lantern signaling the wagons into an arc between the Deschutes and the cañon wall.

Helping with the tents, Lee heard the *swash* of the water and the *clatter* of camp-making, saw the pinpoints of lantern light by which the Harriman men worked with picks and shovels. A sudden slackness had entered into him as if he had stepped out of a cross-whipping gale into a pool of quiet. He felt admiration for this crew that, having come through the shadow of death, now went about its work with the nonchalance of men going through the routine of an average day.

In the morning six men were detailed to

start digging in the tongue of land about seventy-five feet from the Harriman crew. Lee strolled through the camp and on to where the Harriman men were working at the north portal of the tunnel. One of the Porter teamsters was ahead of him, a Winchester cradled over his arm. Three Italians straightened and, seeing the rifleman, dropped their shovels and ran toward the camp.

"Come back here!" a man yelled.

"We wanna da mon!" one of the Italians shouted. "Don't want no lead in da belly."

The man who had yelled wheeled toward the rifleman. "What in hell's your idea of packing that Winchester around here?"

The teamster grinned insolently. "You know how it is when a camp's being set up. Things get lost plumb easy. I wasn't figgering on giving your men any lead in the belly."

"You scared 'em enough to think so." The man's stubbly face grew ugly. "Just one more funny move out of you and your bunch, and the Deschutes is gonna make you damned wet."

"Get back to camp," Lee told the teamster curtly. When the man had gone, Lee added: "Sorry. That fellow had no orders."

"Orders or not, we've lost three of our

men. But if you think that kind of business will keep us from building a tunnel, you're crazy."

"That's not our kind of business," Lee murmured, and returned to camp.

"We're taking the wagons back to Grass Valley," the wagon master told Lee.

"I'll go back with you. Doesn't look like there'll be any trouble here for a while."

They pulled out of the cañon and came into the unshaded sun's brightness atop the plateau. Lee laughed at the look of relief he saw on Baldy's face. He said: "You aren't seeing ghosts, Baldy."

"I wasn't worried none. I didn't hear no blasts go off, so I knew you'd get back if you hadn't fallen off or if they didn't toss you into the river."

"Our trouble will come here," Lee said, "and maybe right away."

It was well after noon when two Twohy wagons pulled up at the gate, a teamster calling: "Open up!"

"You can read the sign, can't you?" Lee said sharply.

"No spikka da English," the teamster grunted. "We want through."

"No savvy da lingo," Lee said. "Stay on that side of the fence."

But the wagons remained where they

were, and Lee moved back to the tent where Baldy stood behind down-thrown flaps. Lee said softly: "Something coming up, but don't know what it is yet. Keep your eyes peeled."

Lee saw, a moment later. A car rocked over the rough road, and ground to a stop beside the gate. A short, fat man stepped down and moved toward the fence.

"Judge Twohy," Baldy said. "I've seen him in Grass Valley. The men in the car are the construction engineer, Brandon, and their lawyer, Bowerman."

Mike Quinn was not in the party. Lee, probing his mind for some explanation of the Irishman's absence, could find none. "I'll see what Twohy's got on his mind," he murmured.

Judge Twohy was angry, thoroughly and completely angry, but he spoke courteously when Lee came up. "This is our road, and you have no legal right to lock this gate."

"It's locked," Lee said laconically. "Let the courts decide our legal right."

"The problem is immediate," Twohy said. "It is not our intention to haul materials down. At the present time we have enough of an outfit in the cañon to complete ten miles of work." He motioned toward the wagons. "They're loaded with food. Whatever motives may have inspired this move, it surely was not to starve three hundred men to death."

Lee reached for his pipe and automatically began filling it, his eyes on Twohy's face. "As far as your wagons are concerned, my orders are clear. I'm not to let them through. On the other hand, I wouldn't try to stop them if you cut the wires."

"We will not do that."

"Or I couldn't stop you if you overpower me and take the key to the padlock."

"Neither will we do that." Twohy wheeled back to one of the wagons. "Toss a quarter of beef over the fence. They can come up from below and get it." He stamped back to the car and got in.

Lee watched in silence while the quarter of beef was thrown across the fence onto the Girt property. Then, as the driver of the automobile got out to crank it, Lee said loudly: "I forgot to lock that lower gate when we came through. Baldy, run down and lock it."

Lee saw Twohy turn. And just before the motor roared to life, he asked: "Bowerman, how long do you suppose it would take us to get a road condemned through this property?"

Lee lost the answer in the *clatter* of the

engine. The car rolled away, the wagons following. When Baldy returned, Lee motioned toward the quarter of beef. "Looks like we'll have fresh meat tonight."

Baldy winked. "Right nice of the Twohys giving it to us."

In late afternoon another Porter wagon train came through, a large group of Italian laborers with it.

"We'll need these men," Lee said to the boss, "if the Twohys try to bust through."

"I'll send them back in the morning," the man said. "We'd better get camp set up on the river before night."

Near evening Highpockets rode in, a great hand waving in jovial greeting when he saw Lee. "Unlock that gate and let me in before I starve to death. I'm so dad-burned hungry. . . ."

"I know. Your hollow leg."

"Sure glad to get that call," Highpockets said as he pulled gear off his horse. "I told the stage company to go jump into the Deschutes, and hightailed it out of Shaniko. Got news," he added. "I hooked onto some newspapers in Grass Valley. *The Dalles Chronicle* says Johnson Porter claims the Harriman outfit wanted to buy them out, but he says they wouldn't sell for five million dollars."

"Sounds pretty big." Lee reached for the papers.

"That there *Bend Bulletin* says something about Johnson Porter claiming the Oregon Trunk's right of way came before anything the Harriman people have got, and the Harriman bunch is just doing a dog-in-the-manger stunt. He says Harriman never intended to build up the Deschutes, and allows they figgered on coming in from the south and throwing all our traffic toward San Francisco."

"I hope Hanna reads this," Lee said dryly.

"She will. And another thing. Quinn set out for Condon in his auto."

"What for?"

"Judge Butler is there, so you can guess."

"An injunction?"

Highpockets nodded. "That's the way I'd call it. Oh, yes, Jepson is in Shaniko."

"Deborah?"

"She's there, too."

Lee swore softly. "What would they be doing there?"

"I wouldn't try guessing on that, son."

After Highpockets had gone to bed, Lee sat beside the fire, smoking and thinking, and arriving at no conclusion. He thought about the bushwhack attempt, and about Cyrus Jepson, and finally his thoughts came

177

to Deborah Haig. His pulse quickened, and he let his dreams build.

Suddenly the *rattle* of a wagon broke across Lee's thoughts. Instinctively he kicked out the fire, and fell back into the darkness toward the tent. He could see no reason for a Porter wagon coming through at this time of night, nor was it likely the Twohys would try again. He called softly: "We've got company."

He heard a stirring in the tent, and Baldy cursed. The wagon was close to the gate now. Lee could make out the black outline of it and the horses. A dark-garbed man moved down from the seat, and called: "Open up! This is a Twohy wagon going through."

"You're not going through." Lee stepped to the front of the tent. He whispered: "Get around to the other side, Baldy. Give High-pockets a Winchester."

"You're asking for trouble!" the man at the gate shouted. "Us Twohys ain't gonna stand for no more monkey business."

Baldy had slipped out of the tent and on around it to the opposite side of the wagon. Highpockets followed him for fifty feet and stopped. Lee held his silence, keeping his position by the tent.

"You unlock that gate, or we'll cut some

wire," the man snarled.

"Don't try that." Lee's cocked gun was in his hand.

Silence, then, a silence that ran on like an endless ribbon. Lee caught the motion of another man behind the wagon, a vagrant gleam of starlight glistening on a rifle barrel.

There was the snip of wire cutters, the lash of a taut strand as the tension was released, and Lee laid his first shot above the man's head. Both men at the wagon fired, bullets droning past Lee and slapping through the canvas of the tent.

Highpockets and Baldy opened up, foot-long tongues of flame stabbing the darkness. The man with the wire cutter cried out, and climbed into the wagon seat. Lee drove another bullet into the body of the wagon directly back of the seat, and dropped flat on his face as lead from the second man's gun screamed over him.

The wagon turned, and Highpockets raised a great cry: "Get down and fight, you sons of Satan!"

The horses were running. The man who had been behind the wagon had climbed into the back, and he emptied his gun now, wild bullets that sang distantly into the night. Then darkness and distance swallowed them, and there was no sight or sound of the wagon.

"What do you reckon the game was?" Highpockets asked as he came up.

"I don't know." Lee kicked up the fire and, when a small flame was building around the juniper, rose, and, ejecting the empties, thumbed new loads into his gun. He said thoughtfully: "I'm just damned sure of one thing. That wasn't a Twohy wagon."

Early the next morning the Italian laborers came up the road from the cañon and spread out across the field back of the tent.

"Any guns in your outfit?" Lee asked the boss.

"No." The man's white teeth flashed in a wide grin. "Pick handles, but no guns."

"That's good," Lee said. "We'll need some pick handles today if I don't miss my guess."

Lee was standing at the gate when the Twohy wagons came into sight, Mike Quinn riding in front, the sheriff and a deputy with him. Lee had sent Baldy back to Grass Valley to report to the Porters' office. Stationing Highpockets in the tent with a Winchester, Lee lined the Italian laborers up inside the fence, and waited.

The look on Mike Quinn's face was one of malicious triumph. "We're back, Dawes, and this time the law's on our side."

180

"That so?" Lee asked indifferently.

"I've got an injunction signed by Judge Butler," the sheriff said. "It says you've got to allow free use of this wagon grade leading from Grass Valley to the Deschutes. Now I'm hoping you'll unlock that gate and not kick up a lot of trouble by defying the law."

Lee's grin was a quick, wide flash across his dark face. He turned the key in the padlock, and pulled the gate clear of the road. "The minute you bring your wagons through this gate, you're trespassing, injunction or no injunction. Remember that, Mike."

Quinn reined his horse out of the road, suspicion setting up a sharp brightness in his gray eyes. Lee stood at the end post, sensing the suspicion in Quinn, and enjoying it. Then Quinn, shifting in his saddle, motioned for the wagons to roll through the gate.

Lee held his silence until the last wagon had cleared the gate. Then he said sharply: "You're on the Girt place now, Quinn, and not with Porter Brothers' permission." Lee signaled to the Italians.

With military precision they broke into bands, each taking a wagon. Moving unexpectedly and swiftly, they overpowered the teamsters by sheer force of numbers, pulled them off the wagon seats and propelled them through the gate. Others unhitched the horses and drove them after the teamsters. The remainder pushed the wagons down the road toward the lower gate.

"You can't do this!" the sheriff cried. "You . . . !" He licked his lips, looked at Quinn, and subsided into speechless agony.

"I should have expected this when I saw your army," Quinn said in ill-suppressed fury. "I suppose you're stealing our supplies."

"We don't steal," Lee said mockingly.

"*Aw,* hell, a man who'd steal a road would steal supplies. If this job takes an army, we'll get an army." Quinn whirled his animal, and rode off, the sheriff and deputy with him, the teamsters mounting and following with the horses.

"They'll be back," Highpockets said gloomily. "You ain't won this ruckus."

"No, but we've worried them and we've kept them out another day. Every day's important in this kind of a race, Highpockets. While we're tussling over this, Porter Brothers is running materials and men into other spots where our surveys conflict. One day here might mean we'll win somewhere else."

"Hadn't thought of it that way," High-pockets admitted. "What are you gonna do with them wagons, run 'em over the cliff?"

"No. They'll string 'em along our west fence."

The Italians stayed on top that night, wagons hauling food and bedding from the cañon.

It was another cloudless day, the sun beating down upon the open country with pitiless abandon. Lee, keeping his usual position at the gate through half the morning, saw the Twohy party coming. Quinn and the sheriff were in front, twenty mounted men behind them, ten wagons bringing up the rear.

"Wonder how Mike figures on twenty men busting through here," Lee mused. He nodded at the Italians, who immediately spilled out across the road.

"We're going through this time, Dawes!" Quinn called as he rode up.

"You said something like that yesterday," Lee murmured.

"If it takes an army to open that damned gate, we've got it."

Lee laughed. "Is that what you call an army, Mike?"

Quinn swung down, not answering, and

183

motioned to his men. "Pick handles in that front wagon, boys. Help yourself." He nodded cheerfully at Lee. "These fellows are deputies, Dawes, in case you're interested."

Lee studied Quinn with puzzled eyes. Mike Quinn had been through too many fights like this to think his twenty men could smash a passage through Lee's Italians. He said slowly: "You're a fool if you slaughter that bunch, Quinn."

"A fool?" Quinn laughed softly, an arrogant certainty about him. "If you think I'm a fool, take a look behind you."

Lee wheeled. Surprise ran through him, and then momentary panic. Hundreds of men had come through the lower fence and were striding swiftly toward the party at the gate, grim purpose on their stony faces. Pick handles, crowbars, shovels — all made a ragged fringe across the front of the crowd. The entire Harriman outfit in the cañon had come up the grade to take part in this finish fight.

Lee picked up a length of juniper limb that lay in the grass, and faced Quinn. The panic was gone now, his lips drawn flat and tight against his teeth. He said: "Looks like we'll have some heads cracked, and, boy, I sure aim to get yours."

CHAPTER TWELVE

Mike Quinn's rugged face showed amazement, and then anger. "You've always been a fighting fool, Dawes, but I didn't think you were so long on the fool part of your make-up."

"Come ahead," Lee invited.

"Don't think we won't."

"Hold on." Highpockets raced across the road in his leggy stride. "Don't start no fireworks yet, fellers. Somebody's coming."

Lifting his gaze past Mike Quinn and the sheriff's party, Lee saw a horseman coming at a fast pace from Grass Valley, and, from the way he rode, there could be no doubt that urgency was in the saddle with him. Then Lee saw that it was Baldy.

"I don't care who's coming!" Quinn shouted belligerently. "Open up!"

"I know this man," the sheriff broke in. "We'll wait."

Quinn swore angrily, pounding his pick

handle on the post at the end of the gate, but he made no hostile move.

Baldy thundered past the wagons and pulled up at the gate, reeling a little in the saddle from the violence of his ride. He ran a sleeve across his dirt-smeared face and, leaning over the gate, said in a low tone: "Johnson Porter saw Quinn leave with the sheriff's party, and him and the rest of 'em decided it wasn't good business to hold the gate any longer, till we get the injunction dissolved."

For a moment Lee stood staring at Baldy, the sickness of defeat in him as his mind gripped this new order. Slowly he nodded and, drawing the key from his pocket, opened the padlock.

"So they pulled off their dogs," Quinn sneered.

"Just tied 'em up, Mike." Lee handed another key to Baldy. "Ride down and open the lower gate." He swung the wire gate away from the road, and motioned for the wagons to go through.

The Harriman laborers fell back, and, after a moment's consultation with Quinn, retreated into the cañon. Quinn waited at the lower gate until the wagons were through and had dropped on over the rim. Then he rode back to where Lee was standing beside the sheriff's party, his smile a mocking whiplash for Lee.

"They'll pour enough supplies over this road in the next few days to lay twenty miles of steel," Lee said sourly as he watched them go, "but so will we. Highpockets, you'd better stay here. Just keep an eye on what goes through."

Returning to Grass Valley with Baldy, Lee reported to Johnson Porter what had happened, and rode north to Moro. He sought out the county judge, and asked: "How long will it take Twohy Brothers to get a road condemned through the Girt place?"

"Hard to say," the judge answered. "Perhaps six months."

Lee took a room in the Moro Hotel, and remained there through the week, the scene of battle shifting to the courtroom. Judge Butler had come by train from Condon to hear cause why the injunction should not stand. The next morning, H. S. Wilson, Porter Brothers' lawyer, moved that the temporary injunction secured by the Harriman lawyers be dissolved. Wilson asked for a quick trial, calling attention to the fact that Porter Brothers had come into court immediately.

Bowerman, one of the lawyers for Twohy

Brothers, argued that Monday would be the first day they could get their witnesses together. Later, he agreed that, if Wilson would put the farm owners on the stand, Friday would be all right for the hearing. Wilson answered that he did not know the farm owners personally, but it would be agreeable to him for Bowerman to get them and ask any questions he wished. Judge Butler set Friday for the case to be heard.

"We'll get it dissolved all right," Wilson told Lee confidently that noon.

The lawyer was proved to be a good prophet when Judge Butler did dissolve the injunction, holding that the evidence did not prove that the Twohys had secured any right to cross these ranches. The Harriman attorneys started proceedings to condemn a road, a fact that did not particularly worry Lee, but he rode back to the Girt place without the feeling of triumph the legal victory should have given him.

"What's been going on?" Lee asked as he reined up at the gate.

"Never saw so much freighting in my life," Highpockets answered. "Been some Porter stuff through here, too, but you ought to see what the Twohys have been doing. I don't reckon they've had a wagon that's stood still since Quinn brought that first bunch through."

"They'll stand still now," Lee said grimly, and locked the gate. "I don't reckon Mike will give us any more trouble trying to get through here."

When Lee saw that the Twohys had accepted the court decision, he returned to Grass Valley with Highpockets, leaving Baldy at the gate.

"You did a good job," Johnson Porter told Lee. "It was a delaying action, and it worked. What's more, we've got a road to use." He laughed. "I'll have to get out there someday, and watch them take hay down on mule back."

"What about our side of the thing?"

"No complaints. Stuff is coming into The Dalles in fine shape. *The Bailey Gatzert* got in with fifteen tons of equipment . . . sledges, anvils, coal, axes, shovels, and whatnot. We're sending most of it to Dufur on the Great Southern, or part way to Boyd, and from there it isn't so bad to freight it into the cañon. We're sending some on to Sherars Bridge, and we're shipping an outfit of heavy equipment we had stored at Vancouver . . . dump cars, steam shovels, rails, locomotives."

"How do we stack up with the Twohys on manpower?"

"They're a little ahead of us," Porter admitted. "They've got about twelve hundred men at work. That's more than we have, but we're pulling them in fast, and we'll be working all along the cañon."

"Horses?"

"We've got about fifteen hundred, and we're buying more."

"I was asking because I'd like to pull off another delaying action somewhere along the line," Lee said thoughtfully. "If we could corner all the horse feed in the country, we'd worry them some more."

"It's worth a try," Porter agreed. "Go ahead. For the moment we can let the Girt place stand. I want to send you south again, anyway. Take Magoon with you." He turned to a map on the wall. "Notice where Willow Creek comes into the Deschutes. Right there is three-tenths of an acre next to the river that could block us. We've got to have it."

"I'll get it," Lee promised.

Porter brought his finger down the black line that was the river. "We cross to the east side here. Between this point and the mouth of Trout Creek our surveys are in conflict. We've protested to the General Land Office, basing our argument on our priority of right at that point."

"Stacks up like trouble."

Porter nodded. "It is trouble. Right now we're fighting in Portland in the courts. The Harriman legal forces claim we've filed old maps that have been bought, illegal surveys, and all that with the Interior Department." He gestured angrily. "They won't make it stick, but it's one of those things that makes railroad building tough."

Lee and Highpockets took the train to Shaniko, and Highpockets, securing the same team of bays that had taken Lee on his first trip into the interior, drove again across Shaniko Flat, down Cow Cañon, and into Madras.

"I know this fellow on Willow Creek," Highpockets said. "He's been as balmy as the rest about the people's railroad, but I've got a hunch he'll deal." He hesitated, pulling thoughtfully at a huge ear. "I'm thinking a lot of folks are going to change their minds when they see what's happening in the cañon."

"Hanna maybe?"

"Well now, I wouldn't be sure about her. She ain't a filly you can hold back once she takes the bit into her teeth."

Highpockets was right about the Willow Creek property. The farmer said frankly that a Harriman agent named Quinn had offered him $3,000 for the vital piece of land, but he hadn't sold.

"I just don't like the idea of playing dog-in-the-manger, mister. We've been looking for a railroad into this country for a long time. Now that we're gonna have two, I ain't a man to try to stop one of 'em. If you want that piece of land and a right of way across my ranch, you can have 'em both for three thousand."

"It's a deal," Lee said quickly, drawing checkbook and pen from his pocket.

Lee and Highpockets returned to Madras that night, and spent several days in the northern part of Crook County determining the practicality of cornering the hay and grain supplies. The last day they swung south to Crooked River, and stopped at Hanna's place on their way back to Madras.

"I suppose you stopped here because Highpockets got hungry," Hanna said.

"He's got hold of the lines." Lee grinned as he stepped down and patted Willie. "Come to think of it, I've got a hole in my stomach, too."

"Come in. We'll see what we can do about filling it. I've got some newspapers to show you. Or have you kept up on the developments?"

"No. I've been traveling too much. Seems like the reporters know more about my railroad than I do."

"Don't you get her to talking and hold up supper," Highpockets warned as he unhitched and led the horses to the water trough.

Lee followed Hanna into the kitchen, and grinned when she said: "At last the big secret is out. The *Bend Bulletin* reports that Jim Hill is backing the Oregon Trunk."

"It was time to tell it. I hear that a Bend newspaperman was chasing up and down the cañon trying to find out who was backing the Trunk, and just when he did find out and thought he had a scoop, Stevens gave out his statement."

Hanna laughed. "Well, it just goes to prove that there is a strange element called luck that plays a big part in our lives." She picked up a newspaper from the table. "This *Madras Pioneer* just came today. It quotes from *The Dalles Chronicle* to the effect that central Oregon's sympathies are with Hill, because Harriman has a record of broken promises."

Lee reached for the paper, eyes scanning the editorial. He muttered: "The Columbia Southern would have been extended south if Harriman hadn't bought it. The Corvallis and Eastern would have come in, but Harriman got that. The passes from the south are controlled by Harriman. Central Oregon is bottled up. All but the Deschutes route." He tossed the paper back on the table. "More Harriman Fence which we're going to break down. Hanna, I could talk a week, and I couldn't give you any stronger reasons why you should sell us a right of way."

She gestured wearily. "Some of my neighbors are going to see it that way."

"She's weakening, son!" Highpockets called from the doorway.

Lee, watching her, was not sure. There was a firmness of moral fiber, a strength of character in her, that would not let her change a decision this easily. "I hope you are weakening," Lee said gravely. "A lot depends on you."

"I know." She turned into the pantry, calling back briskly as if putting the railroad question out of her mind: "I'm out of wood! No wood, no eat. A couple of tramps like you ought to work for your meal, anyhow."

"Sure," Lee said. "Where's the woodpile?"

They returned to Shaniko the next day, Lee riding most of the way in silence, thinking of the possibilities that control of the local supply of hay and grain would give the

Oregon Trunk, and seeing the difficulties involved in securing such a monopoly.

That evening, as Lee and Highpockets crossed the lobby of the Columbia Southern Hotel and entered the dining room, they met Cyrus Jepson.

" 'Evening, Dawes," Jepson said pleasantly.

"Howdy. What's going on in Jepson City?"

"Development, Dawes. Nothing can hold that country back. We'll have the biggest irrigation project in Oregon around Jepson City."

"I thought it was desert."

"Desert today, Dawes. A Garden of Eden tomorrow."

"You reckon Eve got that apple off a clump of sagebrush, Jepson?"

The little man jabbed a slender finger at Lee. "We won't have sagebrush around Jepson City. We have a lake to turn into the desert, Dawes, and with an unlimited water supply, the desert will grow anything. Anything. If you're looking for an investment that will return you tenfold, don't pass up Jepson City."

"Save your promotion talk for the boomers, Jepson," Lee said.

"I have plenty for them." Jepson drew a cigar from his pocket, round eyes on Lee.

"I've liked you, Dawes, from the moment I first talked to you at Biggs. I'd like to see you come in on something that's good."

"If you've liked me," Lee said with biting irony, "you have a strange way of showing it."

"What do you mean?"

Lee saw he had made a mistake. There was no way to prove what he suspected, and the only way to get the proof he needed was to let Jepson extend himself so far that he had to come into the open. So now Lee shrugged and said — "You haven't been very friendly to the Oregon Trunk, Jepson." — and moved on to where Highpockets had taken his seat at a table.

"Opportunity don't knock more'n once, son," Highpockets said, and winked. He whittled on his steak, and then added: "Oh, I forgot to tell you. I saw Jepson and that black-haired Haig filly in the parlor upstairs. They were sure talking a blue streak. I'll just bet she's fixing to slit Quinn's throat."

Lee had not seen Deborah for weeks, but the fire that the first sight of her had lighted in him had not died. His thoughts turned to her, and he felt the poignant stab of desire as the image of her dark, exotic beauty filled his mind.

"You see that picture of a submarine

called *Snapper?*" Highpockets asked. "In *Popular Mechanics,* I think it was."

"No."

"Dad-burned funny thing. Going under water. Going up in the air like them Wright brothers. Going on land in autos thirty, forty miles an hour. Sometimes it plumb scares me what'll happen next."

"I know. I'm going to get me some earplugs."

Highpockets sobered as Lee's meaning reached him. He said — "Oh." — in a hurt tone, and lapsed into silence.

Lee asked at the desk for Deborah's room number, and tapped on her door. There was no answer, nor did he hear any sound in her room. She did not want to see him. Her actions had made that plain, but he did not understand it. He walked the streets for a time, had a drink, and, returning to the hotel, tried her door again. Still there was no answer, and he went along the hall to his room. He lay awake a long time staring into the darkness, while the raucous street rackets of the brawling boom town slowly died.

Lee and Highpockets took the train to Grass Valley the next morning, Lee going immediately to Porter Brothers' office, but, before he made the turn into the building, he heard Mike Quinn call: "Dawes!"

Waiting for Quinn to come up, Lee saw that the big Irishman was angry. Lee smiled a little, thinking that Quinn had been angry most of the time lately. "How are you coming with the Racine property, Mike?" he asked.

Quinn made no answer to the question. He cuffed back his hat, stopping a pace from Lee, his meaty shoulders hunched forward in the menacing posture that was characteristic of him when he was thoroughly angry. "Dawes, you've pulled some sneaky tricks, but this one is the lowest," he said. "The Porters ought to put you to digging wells."

"What the hell are you talking about?"

"You never heard of labor agitators, did you? You never sent 'em into our Horseshoe Bend camps, did you?"

"No!" Lee shouted indignantly. "That isn't our way any more than it is yours."

"For all your cussedness, Dawes, you didn't used to be a liar." Quinn's craggy face reflected the violence of his feelings. "You're sure lying now. Those fellows have raised hell. Got the men worked up about their grub. Told 'em we'll starve 'em, because you've blocked off our road. They keep harping about how dangerous the work is, and they aren't getting enough pay. Then somebody rolls some rocks down to make what the damned wobblies say look good."

"We've had no hand in it, Mike," Lee said. "That sort of business could kick back on us."

Quinn shook a hard-knuckled fist under Lee's nose. "Then if you didn't have no hand in it, why are our men going over to your camp?"

"I don't know." Automatically Lee lifted his pipe from his pocket and filled it, his mind reaching back over the last few days. "Mike, some things have been happening to us that don't jibe with your kind of fighting, and I've held back till I found out who it was. Now suppose you do the same."

Lee wheeled into the building, leaving Quinn staring after him.

Johnson Porter, watching the scene through the window, chuckled. "What's biting your Irish friend?"

Lee told him. Porter shrugged, and dismissed it with a wave of the hand.

"Any good come of your trip?"

"We've got the right of way through that Willow Creek property, but it doesn't look like we'll have any luck cornering the horse feed. Too much of it."

"I've got a letter for you." Porter moved

back to his desk and, thumbing through some envelopes, found the right one and handed it to Lee.

Lee tore it open, and read the brief note.

Portland, Oregon
August 20, 1909

Dear Dawes:
You did a fine job with the Girt homestead, and Johnson's reports on your work are satisfactory. On the other hand, you have not yet secured the right of way across the Racine property. You've had the time you asked, and it should not be necessary to remind you that we will not build into Bend if we cannot bridge Crooked River.

Sincerely yours,
John F. Stevens

Lee raised his eyes to Porter, and grinned wryly. "Guess I'm not doing so well."

"Woman trouble?" Porter asked.

Lee nodded. "I wish John Stevens would argue with Hanna Racine. Just once. Then he'd know why I haven't got the right of way."

CHAPTER THIRTEEN

Late in August, the Oregon Trunk won the first round of the bitter legal battle that was being waged in the Portland federal courts — an injunction restraining the Deschutes Railroad Company from molesting the Oregon Trunk at any point where the two roads had been disputing for equal right on the upper sixty miles of the survey. This decision, handed down by Judge Bean, gave the Oregon Trunk undisputed right to that section of the cañon, and it was a bitter blow to the Harriman forces.

The immediate effect of Judge Bean's decision was to bring about a cutting down of the Harriman crews. Sixty-four men were laid off by the Twohys, and given free passage on the OR&N to Portland, so that the Porters would not hire them. Johnson Porter, hearing of the incident, contacted his Portland agent, and announced that the men would return to work for Porter Brothers.

"From the reports I've received since I returned here Tuesday night, the Harriman camps appear like a Quaker meeting on a Sunday morning, all quiet," Johnson Porter told a representative of *The Dalles Chronicle.* "I am hiring all the men they discharge as fast as I can, and am getting as many more as can be obtained. We have a standing order in Portland for one hundred and fifty men to be sent out every day."

Lee Dawes left Grass Valley for the Girt place the morning the news of Judge Bean's decision reached Porter Brothers' office. Leaning back in his seat, and puffing steadily on his pipe, he felt optimism boil to a new height in him. Highpockets watched him for a time. Then he said: "You're feeling so dad-burned good you're about to sprout wings and take off. Strikes me you're laughing a mite soon."

"Hell, they can't build a railroad without a right of way."

"Which they'll get, one way or the other. I heard about a Hill big gun saying that, if the Harriman bunch would stay on the east side of the river, they'd stay on the west side, and both of 'em could build all the road they wanted to."

202

"That was said all right," Lee admitted, "but even if we relocate on the other side here at Horseshoe Bend instead of tunneling, they'll run into trouble down there below U'Rens's ranch where we swing over to the east side. Looks to me like we've got 'em licked if they don't pull a rabbit out of their hat."

"What are we coming out here for?"

"To see if Baldy's having any trouble at the gate." Lee knocked his pipe against the side of the buggy. "I figured I'd go on down into the cañon just to see if they're getting ready to quit."

Baldy had the gate open for them, and shook his head in answer to Lee's question. "No trouble here. I mean nothing that amounted to anything. A wagon rolled in last night about midnight, and somebody shot at me a couple of times. When I shot back, they vamoosed. Guess they wanted to play tag."

"Didn't say anything?"

"Nary a word."

"Cut any wire?"

"Nope. Pulled out soon as I squeezed trigger. I walked up and down the fence the rest of the night, but nothing else happened."

Lee sat puzzling about it for a moment.

Finally he said: "It's a damned poor thing to have to fight a shadow."

"Nothing shadowy about them bullets," Baldy said.

"We're going on down, but we'll stay here tonight. If something's in the wind, I want to be here."

"And I'll sure feel better if you are here," Baldy said with evident relief.

They wheeled on across the Girt place, through the lower gate, and down the steep, twisting road to the bottom of the cañon. There had been a slow breeze on the plateau; there was none here. The sun, directly overhead, loosed its rays into the cañon, making a fierce, stagnant heat that brought a burst of sweat out of a man's body and seared his lungs as he breathed.

Highpockets ran a sleeve across his forehead, jerked a thumb at the river, and muttered: "I'll bet the dad-burned thing's a-boiling."

They had their midday meal at the Hill camp. "They've got seven miles that ain't touched by injunction," a foreman told Lee. "They're pushing for all they're worth on them seven miles."

"Then they've got something else up their sleeves."

"They sure ain't quitting. When the gate

204

was open, they ran enough supplies through to last 'em a hell of a long time. They've had some labor trouble, and some of their boys have come over to us, but I never did see no reason for it."

"They haven't laid off any of their men?"

"Not here."

Lee spent the afternoon in the cañon. Several Harriman crews were working along the river, the earth-trembling reports of blasts coming often. Construction rails were down; dump cars filled with rock *clattered* by Lee. There was a city of tents at Horseshoe Bend, crews of men working at both ends of the tunnel.

Lee was treated with cool courtesy. He was told that the tunnel would be eight hundred feet long with a ten-degree curve. Eighty men were being fed at one camp. Another and larger camp had been established two miles above the bend. Here Lee found the biggest commissary he had seen anywhere along the river: cases of canned goods stacked high, huge piles of potatoes, sugar, flour, beans, and other food supplies. Lee, returning to the buggy, had the feeling that the Deschutes Railroad Company was determined to lay steel over as much of the right of way as it could, and that Judge Bean's decision had not lessened that determination.

"Funny some of them fellers didn't bend a pick handle over your head," Highpockets said as they started up the grade. "Or didn't they know you?"

"They knew me all right," Lee said thoughtfully, "but maybe they're playing smart. They don't want us to think they're pulling out yet. Not from this spot anyhow."

They came up out of the cañon, broke over the rim, and spun on across the plateau to Baldy's camp. The sun had dropped low to the Cascades, and a soft west wind from the mountains touched them and gave a pleasant relief after the closeness of the cañon.

"I wouldn't work down there for a million dollars," Highpockets said feelingly.

Lee said little while they ate. His thoughts were busy with the events of the previous evening. It was almost dark now, the last of twilight fading into night, and somewhere along the rim a coyote gave voice to his weird call. Lee rose, and knocked his pipe against his heel. "Baldy, there didn't seem to be any sense to that business last night, and that's why I'm thinking it's some kind of a trick we haven't seen through. Chances are they'll come again tonight."

"Who is this 'they'?" Baldy asked.

"Jepson, of course, and Boston Bull. Some of these freighters are just plain stubborn. I've seen some of 'em who were fool enough to think they could smash a railroad. They'd make a try just because railroads bust up their business."

"And Boston Bull would sure like to stop your clock," Highpockets murmured.

"No doubt of that. Baldy, you stay here at the gate. I'll take the south corner, and, Highpockets, you take the north. Keep moving and listening. If you hear anything out of the way, start shooting."

Lee moved away from the camp, keeping inside the fence. Presently the campfire was lost behind a ridge, and there was only the pit-black night with the far vault of the sky above and the wide earth around him. He reached the corner, and stood there for a long time, feeling the need for his pipe and knowing that he dared not smoke. He came part way back to the gate, and returned to the corner again, standing there while slow minutes plodded by in their march to eternity.

The distant *clatter* of a wagon broke into the stillness. Tensing, Lee searched the eastern blackness and caught no hint of movement. He stood very still, breathing softly, sorting the night sounds that came to him and making a pattern of them. The wagon he had heard was coming directly toward him, but another outfit had veered northward and apparently was heading toward the gate. This puzzled him for a time, and then he saw the trick. The rig headed for the gate was a decoy to take Baldy's mind off the one they meant to slip through.

Whiskey! Lee wondered why he hadn't thought of it before. A bootlegger could do a tremendous business in the cañon now. If Jepson was behind the move seeking to make trouble, he would achieve that end. A wagonload of whiskey could create more disorder in a camp of men whose tempers were already frayed thin by heat and danger than anything else Lee could think of.

Lee stepped back from the fence, drew gun, and waited, and it was then that a rifle shot stabbed the night silence. Somewhere to the north. Just about at the gate, Lee guessed, and instinctively he started toward it, and immediately stopped, knowing it was the wrong thing to do. If this was the wagon they wanted to slip through, it would be the one to stop, and he had neither time to get into the fight at the gate nor seek help.

Presently the dark bulk of a freight wagon lumbered into view, and stopped close to the fence. A man said something in a low tone; a second answered and climbed down. The firing at the gate had increased, and from the sound of it, Lee judged that both Baldy and Highpockets were in it, and that three or four men were in the other wagon.

The man who was working on the fence in front of Lee said: "Ain't far to the rim. The boys'll keep the guard busy long enough to dump this."

Lee lifted his gun and fired, putting his bullet close to the man at the fence. "Stand still and toss your guns over here!" he called. "Let me hear them."

Expecting this to be a finish fight, Lee moved as he spoke, anticipating an answering fire, but none came. The man at the fence gave a scared yell and ran. The one in the seat cursed, the sound of his voice so shrill that it was close to a squeak. He hit the ground, tripped in a snarl of wire, cursed again in a frenzied panic of fear, and, getting loose, raced away into the darkness.

Lee slipped his gun into his holster, and, finding the lines that the man had dropped, stepped up into the wagon seat. The horses, evidently trained to stand at gunfire, had not bolted. They moved now at Lee's command, the wagon rumbling over the rough ground.

Presently the firing at the gate stopped. Lee, following the fence, came to Baldy's camp. "This is Dawes!" he called.

He heard Highpockets's yeasty sigh, Baldy's soft oath of relief as he stepped to the gate to open it.

"Get a lantern!" Lee called. "I haven't looked into the wagon, but I made a bet with myself that the cargo's whiskey. If it is, we'll break open a case. Might be a bottle of pop for you, Highpockets."

"If it's whiskey, we'll unload it right here," Baldy said.

Highpockets brought the lantern from the tent. Lee, throwing the canvas aside, took one look, and felt fear creep along his spine, his nerves tying hot little knots under his skin. He stepped back, and sleeved the sweat from his face.

"Well, crack open a case," Baldy said impatiently. "I'm so dry that every time I spit it turns out to be dust."

"Then you're going to keep on spitting dust," Lee said hoarsely, "because you won't be drinking anything on this wagon. It's loaded with dynamite, and there's a quart of nitroglycerine to give it a boost."

There was a moment of stunned silence, and then Baldy yelled — "Dynamite!" — and scrambled back.

Highpockets didn't stir. He stood pulling at his beard, his face grave and thoughtful. "What do you reckon the game was?" he asked.

"The way I read it," Lee answered, "the wagon that came here and the shooting ruckus they started was to get Baldy's attention, so he wouldn't know anything about this outfit. Probably they aimed to take it down the road a piece and let it go over the edge, so it would wind up in one of the camps. There's enough powder on them four wheels to blow a camp out of the cañon and set it on top."

"And whichever side got it would think the other bunch did the job."

"That's right," Lee agreed. "Baldy, I don't think you'll have any more trouble tonight. I'll tell Porter to send a couple of men out here. We'll tie our horses behind this wagon, and head for town."

"You want me to ride this rig into town?" Highpockets asked sourly.

"Sure. I'll drive, and you can hold the nitro."

"Handle it like a baby," Baldy said.

Highpockets swallowed. "I never did hold no baby, but guess I'll know how by the time I get to Grass Valley."

They rolled into Grass Valley before dawn, got the deputy sheriff out of bed, and left the load of dynamite in his reluctant hands. Taking a room in the Vinton Hotel, they slept well into the morning. It was nearly noon when they walked into Porter Brothers' office.

"The dynamite news is all over town," Johnson Porter said the minute he saw Lee. "What do you make of it?"

"Nothing yet." Lee sat down and tipped back in his chair. "I'm still looking for proof. I could go after the man I think is responsible, but I don't think Stevens would want that."

"No, he wouldn't," Porter agreed.

"So I'll have to let them keep running out rope until they've got enough for us to hang 'em. I'm hoping this is the time."

Porter began walking the floor, his long face tight with worry. "It would have been mass murder. Nobody but a maniac would have tried it."

"Maniac or not, it was a smart play for the sort of job they were driving at. We're going to Shaniko today." He motioned toward Highpockets. "I think my partner

212

can uncover something. He knows the right people, and they'll talk to him."

"I was sending you to Shaniko, anyway," Porter said. "We've bought the Central Oregon Railroad."

"What's that?" Lee asked curiously. "Haven't we got enough railroads?"

"No, we needed one more. It seems that a bunch of Portland men who have a good deal of money invested around Bend didn't see any sense in waiting for Harriman, so they cooked up their own railroad. They did quite a bit of surveying between Madras and Bend a little over a year ago."

"So we've got a survey south of Madras."

"That's it, but there are two spots down there that are as important as they ever were . . . Trail Crossing on Crooked River and the Davidson Ranch. We've got to get around a hill there, or climb four hundred feet higher than we should."

Lee, rubbing fingers over a stubbly cheek, grinned a little, and nodded. "Sure, I know. The Racine property is in there, too."

Porter began pacing again. "That isn't worrying us at the moment, because the Harriman bunch won't grab anything there. They can grab at Trail Crossing if we don't grab first, so we've got to beat them to it. We have material and horses at Shaniko.

The men will go from here on the train this afternoon. They'll leave Shaniko tomorrow morning, and keep going until they get there. You and Magoon will go along, partly because you know the country, and partly because this business last night scared me to death. I'm beginning to expect anything." He leveled a finger at Lee. "Be sure you're armed."

"We will be, and don't worry about your outfit getting lost. Highpockets knows that road better than he knows the way between a steak and his mouth."

Coming into Shaniko that afternoon, Lee wished he didn't have to go on to Trail Crossing. The evidence he sought should be here in Shaniko. It was not likely that the dynamiting expedition would leave Moro or Grass Valley, both of which were flooded with Harriman and Hill men. Shaniko was a more likely point of departure, because it was from here that the outfits freighting into the interior departed on their regular runs. Boston Bull could have left with a load of dynamite without attracting attention, swung west and then north, and, traveling by night, could have reached the Girt place without being seen.

After supper, Highpockets talked with several people in the hotel, the saloons, and the warehouse from which Boston Bull regularly departed. He returned to Lee's room, his bearded face showing puzzlement. "Don't make much sense like we figgered it would, son. Jepson's been in his room on a three-day toot. Drunker'n old Nick. That's the way he does. I've knowed it to happen before."

"Three days would have given him time to sneak out and get back."

"Nope." Highpockets shook his head. "He was in his room. Had his meals regular when he wasn't so drunk he couldn't stand. Empty bottles all over the place. No sir, Lee, I'm just dad-burned sure Cyrus P. Jepson didn't attend no dynamite party."

"What about Bull?"

"He hadn't been seen for a long time till tonight. Pulled in from the south a while ago with his freight outfit."

"Jepson wouldn't go on a drunk when he was pulling off a shindig like this one."

They stared at each other, uncertainty a nebulous thing between them, and Lee muttered: "I'll have a talk with a couple of sheriffs when I get back from Trail Crossing."

"No good," the tall man said quickly. "You ain't got nothing but a bunch of notions that don't make real good sense any way

215

you look at 'em."

Lee grunted, knowing Highpockets was right. He moved about the room, prodded into restlessness by the knowledge that he was no nearer identifying the third party than he was to securing the right of way through the Racine place. He thought of Deborah, of her association with Jepson, and anger built in him. She had tried to pump him in one way or another, and, if he could see her and talk to her, he might be able to reverse the procedure and ferret out the clue he was seeking.

Slouched on the bed, Highpockets watched Lee prowl about the room. "I reckon that Haig girl could help you out," he said.

Lee wheeled on him. "Hell, she won't even talk to me. She must have somebody bring her word when I'm in town, because she locks the door and doesn't even poke her head out."

"Another voice might work," Highpockets said. "She don't know mine so well."

Lee nodded a slow agreement. "We'll bring her a telegram."

They moved along the hall to Deborah's room, neither speaking, and Highpockets drummed urgency into his knock. He said shrilly: "Telegram for Mister Jepson, ma'am.

216

He don't answer when I knock on his door. It's real important. Something about Boston Bull."

There was a moment of silence while Highpockets faded down the hall, then Lee heard light, quick steps cross the room, and the door opened.

"You," Deborah said in quick panic, and tried to close the door, but Lee, putting his weight against it, shoved past her.

Deborah retreated across the room.

Lee shut the door, and stood watching her, a small and mocking grin on his lips. "You must have a peephole so you can see who's out here."

"I've learned to keep a door locked when you're in town."

"You want it that way?"

She stood motionlessly at the window, eyes on the far reach of Shaniko Flats.

"Or were you acting on orders?" He paused, and, when she neither spoke nor moved, he went on: "Quinn's? Or maybe Jepson's?" Still she said nothing. "We're playing a different game from the one I thought we were, Deborah. I'm not just sure about the rules or the stake the winner pulls in. What are they?"

Outside, a step sounded in the hall, and knuckles beat a sharp tattoo on the door.

217

Deborah turned, holding up a hand to silence Lee. "Who is it?" she called.

"Cyrus. I'd like to talk to you, Deborah."

"In the morning. I'm going to bed now."

"It's important." Anxiety and anger honed a keen edge to his voice.

"In the morning, Cyrus."

Silence, then, for a long moment, and Lee heard the little man's heels sound in quick, angry taps as he moved away.

"I heard he'd been drunk for three days in his room," Lee said. "He didn't sound drunk to me."

"It wasn't so," Deborah cried, and caught herself as if she regretted the words. "I mean he's been sick."

"I see," Lee said, and came across the room to her. "The stakes are high in the big game everybody in central Oregon is playing and they're high in this little side bet you and I made when we first talked on the *Inland Belle.* The smart thing now is to show our cards."

Her face was a heart-shaped oval in the dusk, her eyes black dots against the lightness of her skin, her mouth a dark line holding both an invitation and a promise. "What do you mean?"

He laughed softly. "As if you didn't know. I'm talking about the outfit that tried to run a wagon loaded with dynamite through the Girt place last night. Who was it?"

"I don't know."

"Jepson just wanted to talk to you, and you opened the door to me because you thought there was a telegram about Boston Bull. I think they're the ones who pulled off this dynamite party."

"It's a good thing you can't hang a man because of another's thoughts, isn't it, Mister Dawes? You may close the door on your way out."

He would accomplish nothing more against the curtain she had drawn, but he was not ready to leave. He murmured: "There is the little matter of our side bet."

He had that naked sense again as if she were exploring the secret places of his mind, measuring him, searching out and weighing the losses and gains that might come to her from this side bet.

Her voice came low and husky, and without conviction: "I don't think this is the night, Lee."

She said nothing about propriety. It was an old game, and one that Lee Dawes played exceedingly well. He took her hands, warm and long-fingered and magnetic with the urge of life. "I told you in Madras that we were the same kind of people, and you knew it as well as I did. I've played the cat-and-mouse game because that was the way you liked it."

"And now you're done playing." She laughed softly. "I warned you, Lee. I'm bad for you."

"It would be a hard life without some of the things that are bad for us," he said.

"That night in Madras you said something about a fair trade. What do you have to offer?"

"We have something to offer each other," he said quickly, and drew her into his arms.

She was passive for a moment, and then her lips became greedy with the hunger he evoked; her arms came up to fold around his neck, and a wildness was in them both. There was satisfaction here, and shock ran along his nerves and warmed him and told him this girl held all the promise he had felt from the first moment he had seen her.

She drew her lips from his, but remained in his arms for a time, her long body molded against his. "Lock the door, Lee," she said softly.

In another room down the hall from Deborah's, Cyrus Jepson stood at the window pulling fiercely on his cigar, its glow bright red in the dusk. "Hasn't he come out of her room yet?" he asked.

Boston Bull opened the door a crack. "No, he ain't," he said in his thick voice. "What the hell you worrying about? You wanted her to pump him, didn't you?"

"Not at too great a price." Jepson chewed on his cigar, his eyes unseeingly fixed on the street. "She wouldn't let me in her room."

"It's business with you. She's got to work on Dawes different."

"I know." He stood in silence, a little man with a great pride that had been hurt. Then: "It hasn't been just business on my side, and Deborah knows that. It will be different when we finish with the town site."

"We'll never pull any big money out of that town site if we don't get rid of Dawes," Bull said hoarsely. "You ain't smart on that like you are on most things."

"I'm smart enough not to let my feelings throw my judgment out of line. I hate Dawes as much as you do." He paused, thinking of Lee in Deborah's room, and added: "More. But that isn't the point. So far Dawes has had the devil's own luck. Luck doesn't run that way forever, Bull."

"There's no luck about a slug in the guts," Bull said doggedly. "Wouldn't be tough from the rimrock. No evidence to bring 'em to us."

"There are some things you will never understand, Bull, and the results of direct and obvious action is one of them." He took the cigar from his mouth and, holding it out of the window, carefully fingered the ash from it. "We killed Herb Racine because he'd have smashed us if he'd lived. We had no choice. This time we do. The hatred between Quinn and Dawes will grow. Deborah will see to that. She's poison in a man's veins, Bull. I know. And I know what she will do to men like those two. I'm convinced that the only way to do this job is to continue with the tactics we've been following. Once we bring these companies into direct conflict, we'll have no trouble keeping it going." He replaced the cigar and reflectively chewed on it for a time. "Our next step is to work those Austrians up about their beef. You'd better have a talk with Franz before he leaves town. A hundred dollars should be enough."

"Damn it," Bull said angrily, "I don't see no sense in this pussyfooting."

"If we come to the place where we have to kill him, we'll fix it so he'll walk into it. A killing needs as much finesse as you have to use in handling a difficult woman, but we'll not kill until we have to. Understand that, Bull. One smart killing is relatively safe. Two, no. Even more than a year apart as these are, there are some people who would talk and that would set the smart ones to thinking."

"So you use that fin . . . fin. . . ."

"Finesse."

"Whatever it is, you'd better use some tomorrow on Deborah, 'cause Dawes has been in there a hell of a long time."

In a sudden gust of anger, Jepson tore the cigar from his mouth and threw it into the street. He wheeled away from the window, and said sharply: "We'll go to bed. The waiting will do us no good. And perhaps you're right. A well-aimed bullet in a man's guts would finish his luck."

"Yeah," Bull agreed. "It would for a fact."

CHAPTER FOURTEEN

Deborah turned, and regarded Lee sleepily as he pulled on his coat. The sun had cleared the eastern hills along the John Day, and was casting a rectangular crimson pattern on the bed. Deborah's hair, framing her face in sheer black, made a striking contrast with the white pillow.

"Trying to sneak out?" she asked.

"Got to hurry," he said.

"Where to?"

"Trail Crossing," he told her, and immediately cursed himself for a fool. Still, if the men were ready to move, no harm would come from her knowing. "A fair trade?"

"It will help." She was smiling a little, her body long and softly curved under the covers. "No kiss?"

"I've got an extra one." He sat down on the bed, a finger twisting a strand of her hair around it. "Who tried to pull off that dynamite party?"

"I don't know," she answered, meeting his eyes squarely.

He shrugged. "All right. Be stubborn." He kissed her then, and came to his feet. "I won't be gone more than a day or two. You'll be here?"

"Yes, but will you come back? No lies now."

"You bet I'll be back." He grinned. "And no more door locking."

"No more door locking."

He picked up his hat and, moving to the door, stood looking at her, storing in his mind this picture and stirred by it. "Good bye," he said, and stepped into the hall.

They left Shaniko that morning for Trail Crossing, thirty men with four horse teams. Moving at a fast pace, they covered the fifty-three miles in what was something of a record for the rough roads they had to travel. Pulling up at the rim of the Crooked River gorge at 2:00 the next morning, they found no Harriman camp in sight. The race had been won, apparently without opposition. Lee was both relieved and irritated; relieved because he had held his Winchester in his hands all day while he rode the rough, fast-traveling wagon, eyes warily on the rim-

rock; irritated because nothing had happened, and he felt that if he had stayed in
Shaniko, he might have the evidence he
sought.

"Are we going to bridge here?" Lee asked
the next morning as he stood on the rim,
looking across at the jutting rock on the
other side and then down at the stream four
hundred feet below, which seemed at this
distance to be little more than a rivulet.

"They tell me it's the best spot on the
gorge," the foreman answered, "and they're
fixing to throw a bridge across here that'll
be the second highest one in the world."

"I'll take the Deschutes cañon," Lee said.
"At least a man wouldn't fall straight down."

"You'd bounce just once if you fell off
here." The foreman jabbed an expressive
thumb toward the river. "Just once."

Highpockets and Lee were back in
Shaniko that evening, and as Lee came into
the lobby of the Columbia Southern, the
clerk called: "A telegram for you, Mister
Dawes!"

Lee opened it, thinking it was probably
Stevens needling him again about the Racine property or Porter giving instructions
for another job. It was from neither, and

disappointment washed through Lee as he read it.

I had to leave for The Dalles. Will meet you at the Moro Hotel a week from tonight.

Deborah

Lee crumpled the telegram into his pocket, feeling an unpleasant flatness of spirit. He had not realized how much he had been looking forward to seeing Deborah again, how much his dreams had been built around her. He felt a momentary stab of doubt. Had she left because she knew he was coming back? Then the doubt fled. If that had been the case, she wouldn't have bothered sending the telegram.

Lee had his supper and, stopping at the desk, asked: "Is Jepson here?"

"Left on this morning's train," the clerk answered.

"Thanks," Lee said, and stepped into the street, and moved along it to a saloon.

Lee shoved his way to the bar. He saw Mike Quinn a dozen paces along the mahogany from him, and a small grin struck at the corners of his mouth. He had taken Quinn's girls from him more times than Quinn had successfully poached on him, but somehow this was different. There had

227

been no woman back over the years like Deborah Haig. Not for him, and, judging from the warning the big Irishman had given him in Madras, Mike Quinn's feelings were the same. He thought about that warning, and his grin widened. He'd like to see Quinn's face when he heard that Deborah was Lee Dawes's woman, and not Mike Quinn's.

The saloon was packed with the same strange and motley crowd that had been pouring through Shaniko all summer, but there was here, tonight, a greater proportion of railroad men than Lee had seen before, some of them teamsters in town for the night, but most of them laborers on their way to the camps in the cañon. There was a great deal of railroad talk, the bulk of it coming from the farmers and stockmen, and Lee noted with satisfaction that the general run of it held Hill responsible for the present activity in the cañon.

"Ed Harriman just couldn't sit back and see Hill come in here," a grizzled sheepman said.

"Two railroads instead of one," a red-faced homesteader said, "and it suits me. I'm aiming to raise wheat, and I ain't particular which one does my hauling. Mebbe they'll get to arguing, and get the freight rates down."

"Like hell," a Bend locator cut in. "They won't be doing no cheap hauling, friend, but Hill's your man. I say everybody ought to boycott the Harriman outfit. I lived in Bend too long to ever give him any business."

Lee watched Mike Quinn wheel away from the bar, saw his cheeks darken as patience ran out of him. He pushed men away from him until he faced the locator. "Of all the damned fools," he bellowed, "some of you idiots win top prize! Where do you think this state would be if it wasn't for Edward Harriman? You'd be shipping every damned product you raised by freight wagon across the Rockies or by boat around the Horn like your ancestors did."

The locator's laugh was sour. "Seems to me Mister Harriman forgot all about Oregon being in the United States. Ever hear of the Harriman Fence, friend?"

"It doesn't mean a thing," Quinn said grimly. "Harriman would have built in here regardless of the Hill line or the people's movement. Now we're in a hell of a scrap because Hill couldn't sit back and see somebody else make any money."

Anger stirred in Lee Dawes. Stepping away from the bar, he moved toward Quinn, who was facing the mahogany again and pouring himself a drink. Lee said softly: "You bet on the wrong railroad, Quinn." Quinn apparently had not seen him come into the saloon, for he turned now, surprise and then antagonism flowing across his craggy face. Remembering the way Deborah had greeted Quinn at The Dalles, Lee let his anger prod him into saying: "And you've got a way of betting on the wrong woman, Mike."

Quinn held a filled whiskey glass in his hand. For one stiff-muscled moment he stood that way, the whiskey glass in front of him, while suppressed violence brought a twitch to the corners of his mouth. That violence exploded without warning, and he tossed the glass away and lunged at Lee, hard-driving fists seeking Lee's lean face.

Lee dropped back with Quinn's rush, long experience with the big Irishman telling him how the man fought. As if by conscious direction, the crowd in the saloon fell away from covering them. In that first quick retreat, Lee caught the blurred faces of some of the men at the bar — the locator, the homesteader, and others. Then Lee glimpsed the knobby features of Boston Bull, heard his thick-tongued words: "Kill him, Quinn."

Lee was moving back again, and he lost Bull's voice in the crowd's roar.

Always before it had been Lee's way to let Quinn wear himself down. When the keen edge was gone from Quinn and he was short of breath, Lee would stand and fight and batter Quinn into submission. It was not that way now, for patience was not in Lee Dawes this night. In the back of his mind, memory was a red-hot prod stirring him to fury. Mike Quinn had met Deborah before Lee had. They had traveled together, and he wondered if it had been Quinn who had sent Deborah to The Dalles.

These were the thoughts in Lee's mind that brought him to a pitch of fury he had never felt before in any of his fights with Quinn. He backed away only until the first violence had gone from Quinn, and then he stood his ground, trading blows with the Irishman, the meaty impact of fists on flesh running the length of the room — that and the breathing of men the only sounds in the saloon. Lee brought a fist to Quinn's kidney, took a blow into his hard stomach muscles, and answered with a right to the side of Quinn's face, a savage, turning fist that snapped the Irishman's head back. He was hurt. It was there in the sick look that swept his craggy face. Bringing his fists up, he

231

lowered his head and came at Lee as if to butt him in the stomach, a maneuver Lee had never seen him use before.

"You've forgotten how to fight, Mike," Lee taunted as he wheeled aside. "You're getting old. Too old for a pretty woman."

Quinn had no breath to waste in talk. He went on past Lee, carried by the impetus of his charge, and Lee was on him again, sledging him on the head. But Quinn was not as nearly out on his feet as Lee had guessed. He whirled unexpectedly, hands outstretched, and dived for Lee's legs. Lee went down with him, kicking and twisting and trying to get free, but he was unable to bring a punch through to Quinn's body.

Lee rolled away, Quinn after him, reaching for him and trying to get his big hands on him. A weakness was crawling into Lee. Somewhere back along these past minutes he had been hit more times and absorbed more punishment than he realized. He came to his feet with Quinn, battered the Irishman's face with a looping right, and carried the fight to Quinn, knowing Quinn was hurt, and feeling his own need for ending it.

Quinn backed away, and Lee rushed at him just as a man's foot snapped out from the circle, caught Lee's ankle, and dropped him. In that same instant Quinn, electing to stand his ground, drove a vicious right upward that caught Lee's unprotected chin. A million rockets exploded in Lee's head, setting up their red lights in his brain, and, when his lank body hit the floor, it lay without motion.

Lee came to minutes later with somebody sloshing water over him, and with High-pockets shouting in a high, strained voice: "If I ever get my hands on that dad-burned Bull, I'll fix him so his own mama would throw him to the hogs!"

It made no sense to Lee. Not for a time. He got to his knees, the men before him turning as if they were on a red-streaked merry-go-round. He slashed out with a fist.

"Take it easy, son," Highpockets said. "Ain't nobody around here you want to fight. Quinn and Bull are both gone."

Lee came to his feet and lurched to the bar. He poured a drink, and, as he drank it, memory came crowding back into his aching head. Running a hand over his bruised face, he looked at the blood, and wiped it against his pants. "What about Bull?" he asked.

"He tripped you," the locator said. "You had Quinn damned near out, and you were going after him when Bull tripped you. You just fell into Quinn's fist."

"I've been fighting him most of my life," Lee muttered, "and he never knocked me out before."

"No credit to him," Highpockets said angrily.

"He didn't look very proud of himself," the locator said. "He told Bull plenty."

Lee felt gingerly of the back of his head. "Is it all on?"

"All there," Highpockets said.

"Guess I'd better go to bed." Lee took another drink, and reeled back to the hotel.

Lee's head still held a steady, dull ache when he stepped down from the train at Grass Valley the next morning. His left eye was blue and puffy and nearly closed, one corner of his mouth was swollen, and a gash ran along his right cheek. But when he saw Quinn on the street, he managed a grin. The Irishman's face was in worse condition than his own.

"Go on over to the office," Lee told Highpockets.

Lee moved slowly along the street until he met Quinn, sourness at the method of his defeat still rankling in him. He said sharply: "I figured you'd duck when you saw me, Mike. Took two of you to lick me last night."

"For which I'm apologizing," Quinn said

with quick sincerity. "You were crowding me, and I had that punch on the way when you started to fall. Damn it, Lee, I just couldn't stop it."

This was the nearest thing to an apology Lee had ever heard Quinn give any man. He said shortly: "It's all right, Mike. Guess we'll have to get off by ourselves and finish it in our own way."

"Now that's over, I've got something else I want to say. We've got about all we can stomach, Dawes. If you keep up these sneak tricks, there's going to be the damnedest fight in the cañon you ever saw."

"What's biting you now?" Lee demanded.

Quinn shoved his hands far into his pockets. "I kicked the other day about somebody stirring our men up. Now it's rattlesnakes. Somebody got a hundred or more and dropped 'em in our camps. Scared hell out of them Italian boys, and a lot of 'em quit."

"We didn't have anything to do with it, Mike. I tell you it's somebody else who wants us to tangle with each other."

"Somebody else?" Quinn sneered. "And who would it be but you?"

Lee hesitated, knowing Quinn would not believe him but thinking the other should know. He said: "It's Jepson, but he's been too slick so far to get anything nailed onto him."

"That banty rooster?" Quinn laughed sourly. "You're getting hard up for goats to lay it onto, Dawes. I can't hold my men back much longer." He paused, his one good eye bright with anger. "And I'm not sure I want to."

Quinn stomped away and went on into the Twohy Brothers' office. Lee waited until he disappeared, and then turned into the Porters' office. Johnson Porter was there.

He whistled shortly when he saw Lee's face. "Grizzly bear?"

"Quinn bear."

Porter smiled. "You boys going to fight all your lives?"

"Looks like it." Lee told Porter about the rattlesnakes, and added: "One of these days this thing's going to explode, and we've got enough trouble without having a general war on our hands. I didn't find out much in Shaniko, and neither did Highpockets, but I thought I'd spend a few days between the Girt place and Shaniko. I might be able to follow those wagon tracks for a ways. Or there might be a camp those fellows made. Maybe I'll pick up something."

"I was going to send you back to Crooked River," Porter said. "We've got to buy up all the hay and grain we'll need through the winter, and we might as well be doing it now. I thought I'd put you to buying horses, too." He nodded at Highpockets. "You know horses, don't you, Magoon?"

"I know 'em backwards and forwards," Highpockets said. "I'd be pleased to buy for you."

"He's spent most of his life at the back end of 'em," Lee said dryly. He reached for his pipe and moved toward the window, not wanting to go to Crooked River now, because he wouldn't get back for his date with Deborah. And in this moment his date with Deborah seemed the most important thing in the world.

"Magoon can work alone," Porter said. "You go on south as soon as you get done here, Lee. I don't look for any more trouble at Horseshoe Bend."

"Not unless it's stirred up," Lee said. "Did you hear anything about the horses and wagon that had the dynamite?"

"The outfit was stolen several days ago from one of our men who was freighting out of Shaniko."

Lee threw up his hands. "*Aw,* hell, I guess we're up against somebody who's pretty damned smart."

■ ■ ■ ■

The days Lee spent searching the rim of the cañon south of the Girt place were wasted. He traced the wagon tracks to a road, and from there they could have gone anywhere. Moving south toward Shaniko, he rode back and forth across the road in constantly widening arcs, and returned to Grass Valley with mingled elation and depression; elated because this was the night he was to meet Deborah again, depressed because the long-sought evidence was as far from him as ever.

Lee had a shave and bath, and returned to his room in the Vinton Hotel. He dressed quickly, knowing that Deborah would be in Moro now. Even by hiring a rig, he would be late getting there. He hurried across the lobby and into the street, and stopped, not wanting to believe what he saw.

Mike Quinn's automobile had rolled to a stop in front of the Twohy Brothers' office. Quinn was behind the wheel, and Deborah, wearing a linen duster, sat beside him, a veil keeping her hat in place.

A crowd had gathered around the car, and, as Lee came into the street, someone yelled: "Where's the cigars, Quinn?"

"A box of 'em in the office!" Quinn yelled back.

"What's the fuss about?" Lee asked a man in front of the hotel.

"Ain't you heard? Why, Quinn just got married to the best-looking woman in the state. Drove in from Moro just now. We're fixing to give 'em the damnedest shivaree in the history of Sherman County. You'll be around, won't you, Dawes?"

"No," Lee said hoarsely. "I don't guess I will."

CHAPTER FIFTEEN

By early September the battle was joined, not only at Horseshoe Bend, but along the entire length of the Deschutes cañon. It was a strange race, not mile by mile and rail by rail across the continent, as was the historic Union Pacific-Central Pacific contest, but rather an explosion of energy on both sides of the Deschutes.

Always there was the problem of supply. The Great Southern ran to Dufur on the west side of the Deschutes; the Columbia Southern reached Shaniko on the east side of the river. Here in central Oregon, where the last remnant of the old frontier was being shoved aside by the encroaching forces of civilization, these short feeder lines were used to their utmost capacity, but aside from them, the weapons of transportation were those of a former century.

The rivalry between men of the two lines was keen and constant. When the Deschutes was between the competitive crews, nothing more dangerous than words was hurled by one side at the other, these to be lost in the growl of the river. At other times, grading crews worked side-by-side, and often the battle of words turned into a long-range rock-throwing contest. Or fists and pick handles became weapons, and the fight was close and bitter and bloody.

It was like a calling of the nations, these men who fought and transported supplies and hewed a place for the rails from solid rock and laid the steel: Swedish powder men, Austrians, Slavic muck stickers, Italian track layers, Greeks, American muleskinners. Behind them were the men who planned and dreamed and drove: John F. Stevens, Porter Brothers, Engineer George Kyle for the Oregon Trunk; George W. Boschke, who topped the Harriman organization, and the staff of engineers headed by H. A. Brandon. Over and above these two armies, marshaled for the invasion of central Oregon, were the great captains of the rails, James J. Hill and Edward H. Harriman.

It was a restless land, this central Oregon in the late summer of 1909, stirred as if it were a great ocean whipped into movement by a gigantic paddle wielded in some mysterious hand. Regardless of the subtle and far-reaching plans that were hidden in the minds of James J. Hill and Edward Harriman as they reached for empire, the people were on the move.

Moro, Grass Valley, Shaniko, Madras — tiny farming or frontier communities yesterday — were having their moment of glory today. Overnight, they had burst into throbbing boom towns, sprawling over the land in strange, unplanned fashion. Tents were pitched; old shacks long deserted were repaired and mopped and pressed into use; new houses were built, unpainted lumber bright in the summer sun.

Always it was this way as a flood of people followed a battle of the giants, all looking for their own small profit, for their share of the cream to be skimmed from this pool of human restlessness.

Then, on September 9th, word came that Edward Harriman had died at his country home, and Oregon was shocked, as was all the nation and the entire railroad world. He had not been in good health for some time, yet his going was unexpected, and it left a vacant place and brought its doubts to those who looked for the Harriman system to lay steel the length and width of eastern Oregon.

On September 14th, the Portland *Orego-*

nian carried a story stating that ex-Judge Robert S. Lovett, chief counsel for the Union Pacific, had been elected chairman of the executive committee of the company, thereby becoming the successor of Edward Harriman in the control of the vast railroad and steamship systems that the financier had built up. This, the *Oregonian* contended, proved that the Harriman organization was to be perpetuated in just the form in which it had been created.

Lee Dawes had left Grass Valley the day of Quinn's and Deborah's marriage, and had joined Highpockets on Crooked River. He was in Prineville when the news of Harriman's death reached him.

"Funny thing," Lee said thoughtfully. "We've been fighting Harriman's outfit like hell and we'll keep on fighting, but I don't think there's a man with the Oregon Trunk who isn't sorry to hear of his death."

"Even Jim Hill," Highpockets added.

"That's right. For all their scrapping, they held a lot of respect for each other."

Leaving Prineville the next morning, Lee and Highpockets swung up Crooked River to buy horses, and it was late September before they drove their band into Madras. Lee had welcomed the long hours in the saddle, the dreamless sleep under the stars. He tried to put Deborah out of his mind, tried to cut her out of the grip of his memory as completely as a surgeon would cut away an offending member of the body. He told himself over and over that he had not really loved her. She was just another woman that had been his for a moment, and was gone from his life. He should hate her for what she'd done to him, for the promise she had broken. Yet he knew he did not hate her. But when the frozen numbness in his heart began to thaw, he found his thoughts turning more and more to Hanna Racine.

Lee met Deborah on the street the day after he and Highpockets had delivered the horses to a Porter Brothers' camp. Highpockets had remained in the stable to take care of the saddle horses, the liveryman having told Lee that Johnson Porter was at the hotel and waiting to see him. Hurrying toward the hotel, Lee found himself face to face with Deborah as she stepped out of a store.

"It's nice to see you again, Lee," she said gravely.

Lee lifted his hat, hungry eyes sweeping her tall, slender figure, her dark eyes alive and inviting, and anger stirred in him. He said quite casually: "Good evening, Missus

Quinn."

For a moment her eyes were fixed on his lean face, utterly sober as if she was stirred by the same memories that were in Lee. Then she said: "We're living in that little white house at the edge of town." She nodded toward it. "I hope you'll visit us sometime."

"I don't think your husband would welcome my visit," Lee said, and, moving around her, went on to the hotel.

Johnson Porter was eating in the hotel dining room when Lee came in. He waved Lee into a vacant chair. "How did you make out?"

"Highpockets says they're good horses."

"No sign of Jepson or Boston Bull?"

"No, but there will be. Any news I've missed?"

"You knew about Harriman's death?"

"Yes."

"It won't make any difference as far as our railroading goes. They'll battle us just as hard as they have been, but I think we hold a bigger edge than we did. Secretary Ballinger rejected their application for a right of way from Madras down to Sherars Bridge, so we're sitting in the driver's seat as far as the contested ground is concerned. Ballinger held that the Interior Department didn't have jurisdiction to grant their application because it had already approved ours." Porter whittled on his steak. "Of course, there's always that chance of them coming up with a trick we haven't seen. I won't breathe easy until we lay steel into Madras. It's like waiting for lightning to strike. You just can't outguess it."

"I wouldn't be surprised if some of John Stevens's lightning struck me," Lee said ruefully.

"He didn't get anywhere trying to hurry you, so he's decided to give you the time you need. But if you've judged the girl wrong, he'll have your scalp. Right now he's gone East, and I don't look for him back for a month or so. Meanwhile, I've got a job for you."

"More horse buying?"

"No. This fits into one of the original assignments Stevens gave you. That's why I asked if you'd picked up any sign of Jepson or Boston Bull. I think it's more of their work, but if they're as slick as they were on the dynamite job, they won't leave any loose ends for you to pry up." Porter put down his fork, and sat back. "There is this difference, Lee, and it's why I want you to get started in the morning. They're in the middle of their cussedness, and I think you'll move in just in time to split it down the back. We've got our camps set up now, our wagon roads built, our commissary depots established, and we're ready to build railroad. To do that, we've got to furnish meat to a lot of men. We're driving the cattle we've bought to our butchering stations along the rim, and hauling the fresh meat down to the camps. We've been handling about eight thousand pounds of dressed beef a day." He gestured angrily. "That gives our enemies a chance to make plenty of trouble, which they're doing. Two days ago we had a herd scattered all over Shaniko Flat."

"Any clues?"

Porter shook his head. "None. The boys were holding the cattle just above Cow Cañon when a bunch rode in, shooting and yelling, and the next thing they knew those cows took off for the John Day River. Now your job, Lee, is with our camp on the U'Rens's place. The men are Austrians, and they're eating a lot of meat. Lately they've got finicky. They won't eat front quarters. We trade the fronts and hinds back and forth between the camps, so all of them get a fair division, but these Austrians think a cow is made up of all hinds."

"Austrians don't have much meat in the

old country," Lee said thoughtfully. "It might be just a prejudice they've worked up."

"I don't think so. There's a man named Franz, who seems to be the ringleader of the agitation. He doesn't get any better wages than the rest, but several times he's sat in on poker games with some American teamsters and he's had a pocketful of money. He's one of the few who talk good English, and he likes to show off before the Americans. You find out where he gets his money. I want you and Magoon to take a load of beef down tomorrow. It will be all fronts, because they rejected a load yesterday and got pretty nasty about it. Before you're back on the rim, you'll see why I think there's something more to it than just a prejudice."

Lee's grin was quick and wide, and an acceptance of the challenge. "We'll take the beef down," he said.

Lee and Highpockets left Madras that evening, rode north through Lyle Gap and up Cow Cañon, and reined into the butchering station before dawn.

"You're just looking for a chance to grab trouble by the tail," the teamster growled who usually delivered the meat. "Franz is a tough one . . . the kind that's born mean.

Nobody down there can lick him, and he's got the rest of the Austrians scared to hell 'n' back."

"We'll make out," Lee said. "Ready to roll?"

"All set." The butcher patted a canvas-covered quarter of beef. "Lots of good meat here. Dunno why them Austrians are so damned particular."

Highpockets climbed into the seat, and Lee stepped up beside him, a Winchester between his knees. They followed the rim around Big Cove, the early morning air cold and still and touched with the promise of fall, the cañon slowly emerging from purple shadow as the sun rose.

Here, the cañon of the Deschutes was wider, the walls less precipitous. Here and there, rimrock stood sheer and steep above the cañon, but in most places the rim broke off in rounded complacency, evidence of Nature's erosive power where a soft earth gave in to its urgings. The wagon reached the bottom, and rolled on across the nearly level cañon floor. The new grade lay along the river, the earth raw and fresh where men and horses and scrapers had ruthlessly moved it from its centuries-old resting place.

Turning left, Highpockets drove along the grade, the camp within sight of them. Men were idling along the river, and Lee, missing no detail of the scene before them, said: "Nobody's working. They're waiting for this meat wagon, and they're cocked for trouble."

"What's our play?"

"You stay in the seat. Keep the Winchester handy. If Johnson Porter called it right, I'll have to lick hell out of this Franz, and I don't want to get slugged from the back while I'm doing it."

The Austrians had seen the wagon, and were gathering in a solid crowd in front of the cook shack. Highpockets turned off the grade, and pulled up in front of the crowd. " 'Morning, gents," Lee said, and climbed down.

Forty or fifty men were in the bunch, and at the moment Lee couldn't get his eyes on Franz. None of them spoke and none of them moved. Lee had years before developed the ability to size up a crowd like this, and he caught its mood before he reached the rear of the wagon. Anger had built to a man-eating height. If it once broke loose into full violence, Lee and Highpockets would not get out of camp alive. The trick was to single Franz out and settle this individually — a good trick, Lee thought, if he could do it.

Stepping to the rear of the wagon, Lee threw the canvas away from the meat. "You boys waiting to get fed before you start to work?" he asked cheerfully.

No one answered. Lee spotted a man he took for Franz, a squat, great-shouldered figure in the front row. A drooping, yellow mustache covered much of his mouth; his eyes were small and black and without humor. Judging by the way the others covertly watched him, he was their accepted leader, and they were waiting for his orders.

Pulling one of the beef quarters from the wagon, Lee said: "Here's meat, boys. Get your bellies full and go to work." He gripped the quarter and swung it directly at the squat man. "Take it in, feller."

Franz jumped back, letting the beef fall into the dirt. Anger brought a nervous twitch to the right side of his mouth. He said sourly: "I'm Franz. I talk for these men. We won't work unless we get hinds."

"Every cow has two hind quarters and two front quarters," Lee said patiently, as if he were explaining a simple problem to a child. "It wouldn't be right to give one camp all the hinds and make the other boys eat all the fronts."

"To hell with the other camps. We're eating hinds." Franz said something in his native tongue to the other men, and they nodded eagerly. "You see?" Franz brought his little eyes back to Lee. "You give us hinds."

Lee stepped around the wagon until he was within a pace of Franz. He said with cool firmness: "You had hinds last time. Pick up that quarter and pack it inside."

"You try making me pack that meat in," Franz said, the nervous twitch in his mouth twisting the right side of his face into an ugly wickedness, "and I'll kick your guts to pieces."

Swiftly and without warning, Lee was on the man, fists sledging his head on one side and then the other, and Franz went back into the knot of graders behind him. They fell away, surprised at this unexpected audacity. Lee kept on Franz, fists sinking into the hard muscles of his stomach and driving wind from him. He brought his attack back to the Austrian's head and knocked him off his feet with a pile-driving right that caught Franz flushly on the point of his wide chin.

"Stand clear, you dad-burned coyotes!" Highpockets yelled, and fired a shot.

The crowd fell back. Lee heard the rumble of anger break out of them, but he had no time to see what had happened. He understood men like Franz; he knew what the

Austrian would have done if it had not been for the suddenness of his attack. He dropped upon Franz, hard, knees in the squat man's ribs. He heard the *snap* of bone, the *hiss* of violently expelled air. He hit the man on the side of the head, and then on the other, and, seeing that most of the fight was out of him, crawled off and rolled the almost inert body over.

"You ready to pick that quarter up yet?" Lee demanded.

"No, damn you," Franz muttered, and arched his back.

Lee came astride the Austrian, his full weight against the small of Franz's back, and Franz fell flat. Lee grabbed a handful of the man's hair, shoved his face into the dirt, and twisted it in gusty violence. He jerked the squat man's face up from the dirt, still by the hair, and asked: "You want to pack meat now?"

Franz blew out a mouthful of dust, pulled a painful breath back into his tortured lungs, and muttered: "Ja. I'll do it."

Lee stood up, still watchful, while Franz labored to his feet, and wiped a shirt sleeve across his bloody, dusty face.

There was no movement now from the crowd. Their man had been licked, and fight had gone from them. Stooping, Franz picked up the beef and carried it into the cook shack.

Lee followed him closely. When they came out, he asked: "Who paid you to start this trouble?"

"Nobody," Franz muttered.

"You're lying." Lee raised a fist and took a step toward Franz.

"Bull . . . they call him," Franz said quickly. "Boston Bull. Three hundred dollars I got to make the meat trouble."

"All right, Franz. You're done on the Oregon Trunk. Start up the hill."

For a moment Franz made no move. He stood with his shoulders hunched forward, blood dripping from a cut in his right cheek, one eye closed, the other gleaming in a keen wickedness. He said thickly: "I'm done on the Oregon Trunk, but not with you." He swung away and started down the grade.

Lee returned to the wagon. "All right, boys," he said casually. "I guess you'll eat fronts." He pulled another quarter from the wagon, and handed it to a man who took it without a word and carried it inside. When the wagon was empty, Lee said: "You'll get hinds next time, boys." He climbed up beside Highpockets. "Let's roll."

Franz had started up the road when the wagon passed him. Highpockets said with somber unease: "Those boys'll eat fronts all right, but you just made another enemy who likes you about the same as Boston Bull does."

Lee said, fishing his pipe from his pocket: "Franz said Bull gave him three hundred dollars to kick this mess up. I guess that gives me something to talk about when I find Bull."

CHAPTER SIXTEEN

December, and the chill, clear days of fall had given way to winter. The last of November had been entirely wicked, with an early snow in the mountains and a Chinook that had created an unprecedented disturbance in the even-flowing Deschutes. Rising ten feet in twenty-four hours, it became a mud-brown, rampaging torrent. Two of the Twohy Brothers' camps were swept away. One of the Porter Brothers' camps, located on higher ground, was surrounded by water and temporarily deserted because it was impossible to get supplies to it.

The roads across Shaniko Flats and into the cañon were turned into sticky, treacherous seas of liquid gumbo, tenaciously gripping the wheels of loaded wagons, forcing teamsters to put on six horses instead of four. One heavy outfit pulled into the Oregon Trunk camp on the U'Rens's place with thirty-two head of horses in harness.

Then the rains were over, and it froze, and the gumbo roads became as hard as pavement.

It had been a good fall until the rains came, and time had accelerated the race rather than retarded it. The Oregon Trunk relocated its line to the west side from Mile Twenty-Three to the neighborhood of Sherars Bridge. The original survey had called for a crossing to the east side at Mile Twenty-Three and back at Mile Thirty-Eight and a tunneling of Horseshoe Bend. Now, with the relocation, the tunnel was avoided, and Horseshoe Bend was no longer a point in conflict.

John Stevens, making a quick trip into central Oregon, talked briefly with Lee in Madras. "Our difficulty," he said, "if we have any, will be around Mile Seventy-Five where we cross below the mouth of Trout Creek. They opened the road across the Girt place with another injunction, but that isn't important now." He looked at Lee sharply then. "Our other trouble spot is Trail Crossing. What about the Racine girl?"

"She'll come to me when she's ready to deal," Lee said.

"You don't build a railroad waiting for people to come to you," Stevens said with biting irony.

"I'll see her," Lee promised. He got up and paced to the window. It had snowed a full six inches that morning, had stopped, and now, in mid-afternoon, it had started again, a few flakes circling uneasily in the air before coming to rest. Lee watched them for a moment, feeling Stevens's eyes upon him, the impatience that was building in the man. Turning, he said soberly: "I know you think I'm playing this wrong, but I'm positive of one thing. Hanna Racine will deal with us a lot sooner if we don't push her."

"I've let you alone because you seem to understand the situation, Dawes," Stevens said, "but the way things are shaping up, we can't wait much longer. We've started work at Trail Crossing, so the Harriman people can't hurt us unless" — he leveled a finger at Lee — "the Racine girl sells to them and not to us."

Lee, thinking of Hanna's sense of high integrity, said with complete confidence: "She won't. You can count on it."

Lee sat there after Stevens had left for Bend, patiently nursing his pipe, long legs stretched in front of him, a slack-muscled, tall man from whom the love of fighting had gone. Something was missing in him, had been missing since that afternoon in Grass Valley when he'd seen Quinn drive in with

Deborah beside him. It was as if a fire had gone out, the flame and warmth gone, the gray ashes left.

Strangely, as so many times these last three months, his mind turned to Hanna, and feeling stirred in him. The admiration he had felt for her when they had talked on the *Inland Belle* had increased as he had come to know her better, and the thought of her never failed to bring its calm assurance. It was strange, he told himself, for he had always picked the ardent women, the turbulent ones, and Hanna was not one of them. But the past years had been mostly wasted years, and a man could not go on forever wasting them. He had sensed in Hanna depths no man had explored, capacities that even she did not know existed in her.

Then he cursed himself for a fool, and put his thoughts on other things. Hanna Racine would never love him. They were on opposite sides of the fence; they were too different. Then his mind, circling, would come again to Hanna, and he found himself looking forward to carrying out the promise he had made Stevens to see her.

Lee was there when Highpockets came. Stamping the snow from his feet, he saw Lee, and said warmly: "How are you, boy? I was afraid you'd be out looking after the beef business, and I'd miss you."

"I've been up and down that damned cañon ever since you pulled out for Silver Lake," Lee said. "Plenty of trouble, but I never got my eyes on Boston Bull."

"He's been in the desert. I didn't find the horses I wanted at Silver Lake, so swung on north to Jepson City. Jepson was there, and so was Bull."

Interest quickened in Lee. "Reckon they are still there?"

"Jepson ain't."

"How do you know?"

Highpockets put his back to the stove, and held his hands behind him. Then he fingered a big ear, and finally swung back to face the stove. "Jepson's at Hanna's place, and he's doing his best to get her to sell a right of way to Mike Quinn."

Lee stared at Highpockets, unable to believe this. He got to his feet and came to the stove. "She wouldn't do that."

"I'm worried she will," Highpockets said gloomily. "She sets a store by what that slick-tongued coyote says. She's smart in most things, but she ain't smart at all when it comes to Jepson. Reckon it was because Herb liked him."

"She won't sell to Quinn until she's seen

me," Lee said stubbornly.

"I hope you know what you're talking about," Highpockets said with grim doubt. "I laid over at Hanna's place with my horses. Chris, that's her foreman, said Jepson had been there a couple of days nagging her to death."

Lee filled his pipe, a new question rising in his mind that seemed to have no answer. "Why would Jepson want her to sell to Quinn when he's been so crazy about the people's railroad?"

"I sure don't know, but he puts up the argument that a railroad for central Oregon is the big thing, and it ain't so important whether the people build it or Harriman does."

"Hell, why doesn't he want her to sell to the Oregon Trunk?"

"He says the Harriman lines are all around Oregon, so they'd operate cheaper and more efficiently. He claims we oughta think about what's best for central Oregon. Said Hill just started in here to block Harriman."

Lee flamed a match and held it to his pipe. "She won't listen to that argument. She's too smart."

"Hanna's mighty keen on being loyal to her friends."

"How much of a friend is Jepson?"

261

"None, but that don't make Hanna see it."

"You said once you had a notion about who killed Herb Racine."

Highpockets shifted uncomfortably and stared out of a window at the snow, which had begun to fall in earnest now. "I always allowed it was Jepson, but I never could get no reason for it, him and Herb being friends."

"Why do you think it was Jepson?"

"The night Herb was shot I met Jepson coming up the grade. When I got down to the bridge, there was Herb plumb dead. The bullet came through him on about a level, so I figgered he was plugged from the rocks a little above the water. Anyhow, moonlight ain't much good for long-range shooting, so don't reckon he got it from the rim. Of course the killer might have gone up the north grade, but it don't stand to reason Jepson could have crossed the bridge without seeing Herb's body."

"Did Jepson know Herb was going to cross the bridge?"

"Sure. They'd had a powwow in Redmond, and Herb was on his way home. I figure Jepson waited in the rocks a spell, thinking somebody would come along and find the body. I had some ornery horses, so

I was way behind schedule. Reckon he fig-gered I'd gone by."

"You tell the sheriff you saw Jepson?"

"Nope. Being night, Jepson would have said I couldn't see well enough to be sure who it was. He pulled over next to the bank, and I was plumb busy easing my rig by, but I know it was him. I did tell the sheriff to ask Jepson where he'd been, and Jepson comes up with a poker game in Redmond. Had Boston Bull and some more swearing he was there till three o'clock."

"Guess I'd better get out to Hanna's place. I'd like to ask him in front of Hanna where he was the night Herb was killed. Sometimes a man like Jepson schemes so long he gets pulled out kind of fine and gets boogery."

"Are you Dawes?" A man had come in and stood now in the doorway, cold air sweeping into the room.

"I'm Dawes. Shut the door."

The man came across the lobby, leaving the door open, and handed Lee a folded sheet of paper. He wheeled, and walked out, still failing to close the door.

"Damned fool," Lee grunted, and, cross-ing the room, slammed the door shut. "Born in a barn and raised in a sawmill. Say, haven't I seen him before?"

"One of Bull's freighters. He was in that tussle we had in Shaniko."

"Thought he looked familiar." Lee unfolded the note, read it, and handed it to Highpockets.

Written in a fine, Spencerian hand were the words: *I'm in trouble, Lee. Will you help me? Deborah.*

Highpockets handed the note back. "Ain't much doubt about what the trouble is."

"What do you mean?"

"Ain't you seen her? You allus notice it sooner on a purty, slim woman like her than the other kind. Reckon she'll have her baby in two, three months."

"She's married," Lee said sourly. "That's no reason for her to be in trouble."

"Less'n four months. A woman wouldn't be showing in that time."

Lee shrugged. "Nothing I can do for her if she's in that shape. I'm going out to Hanna's place."

"You ain't been around here much," Highpockets said quickly, "and you ain't run into Quinn. He's made some talk about killing you, because you got his wife into trouble before he married her."

Lee pulled on his coat. "If he comes with that at me, I'll beat it down his throat. He's got one coming after what happened in

Shaniko."

Lee had reached the door when High-pockets said: "You're the boss, Lee, and I sure ain't one to tell you what to do, but it strikes me you're overlooking a bet." Lee paused, his hand on the doorknob, and Highpockets hurried on: "I ain't got no idea who the baby's pappy is, but I do know Deborah used to be plumb chummy with Jepson. That's probably why she got that feller to bring the note. Now she's married to Quinn, and chances are she's in trouble with him. She wouldn't be calling on you if she wasn't ready to make a deal."

Lee stood looking at Highpockets, a tight-ness in him that was close to sickness. He wanted nothing more to do with Deborah. She had been a fever in his bloodstream, and now that he had cured himself of that fever, she was sending for him.

"What kind of a deal?" Lee asked roughly.

"She knows plenty about Jepson. Mebbe why he's jumped to the Harriman side of the fence."

"All right," Lee growled. "I'll go see her."

The Quinn house was set away from the town, a small building that loomed darkly now before Lee. He passed a man plodding toward town, shoulders hunched forward, hat tilted low over his face. Lee came to the front door of the house, lifted his fist to knock, and then lowered it. He saw a woman's footprints on the porch not yet covered by the afternoon's snowfall. Beside them was a man's tracks pointing in. Lee thought about this, a warning compulsion sweeping through him.

Dropping to one knee, Lee drew his gun. He remained that way for a moment, listening. He heard nothing inside the house. There was a stillness that seemed to possess the earth, that seemed to flow around him like the passage of a silent stream and left a strange unease in him. Then it came, a man's hollow cough. Lee, putting a hand to the knob, turned it and shoved the door open.

There was a blossom of light as a gun burst into life within the house. The bullet bit a splinter from the door casing above Lee, a second sang through the open space above his head. Lee, catching the vague figure of a squat man against the far wall, fired once, and watched him topple, slowly at first and then, his joints giving way, falling at once, like a down-pulled tent.

He stood in the doorway, attention drawn fiddle-string tight, eyes searching the gloom, the acrid smell of powder smoke biting into his nostrils. Then, crossing to the dead man, he swore softly. It was the Austrian, Franz.

Lee rose, thinking of the implications of this, and then, swinging toward the door, left the room. He had made a full step beyond the porch when the bullet caught him in the chest and knocked him into the snow. There was the beat of the shot against his ears, the blur of the man in the whirling snowflakes. Lee fired, feeling the numbness in his body, and fired again, and suddenly the man wasn't there.

He was on his face, gun falling from lax fingers. Blood came from him, to make a pattern on the snow. Time ran on, unmeasured, and he had a vague feeling that people were around him. Then, cutting through the jumbled impressions that were in his mind, he heard Deborah's voice, far away: "It's Lee Dawes, and he's still alive." And Lee slipped off into a deep blackness, the last thought in his numbed brain that Deborah had invited him to his death.

Chapter Seventeen

They were gray days, filled with strange, vague images that were disturbing to Lee Dawes. He woke in a warm, clean bed. He did not recognize the room, lighted by a single lamp upon a bureau. There was a distorted sense of unreality about all of it that assumed alarming proportions when he saw Hanna standing beside the bed. Her presence was something he could dream about, but he had no right to expect.

Hanna smiled, when she saw that his eyes were open, and gave him a drink. She saw the puzzlement on his pale face, a face that had been so alive and hungry for life. She said reassuringly: "You're in Doctor Coe's hospital in Bend."

He dropped off to sleep. When he woke again, there was a bright sun upon the white earth, and a big man was bending over him. He had lifted the bandage and examined the wound. Now, replacing the bandage, he said: "You've had the luck of the Irish."

Lee scowled. "No Irish in me."

The doctor straightened his thick shoulders and winked at Hanna. "He's got a temper, and that's a good sign." He frowned at Lee. "Irish luck or not, you've had your share. You were just about bled out when I saw you, and you had a bullet hole in your chest big enough to run a horse through. That slug bounced off a rib and plowed up some muscles, but managed to dodge the important stuff." He waved a huge hand at Hanna. "And along with your other luck, you had a nurse who worked twenty-four hours a day."

A woman in the doorway said: "A call just came in from Laidlaw for you, Doctor. A man was dragged by a runaway team."

"All you've got to do is to be quiet, Dawes," Coe said. "From what I hear of you, that's something you don't often do."

After the doctor had gone and Hanna had pulled a chair up and sat down, Lee asked: "What's the date?"

"The second day of January."

"Christmas is gone?"

"It's gone for Nineteen-Oh-Nine, Lee. You were lying there and very near to death."

"I owe you a lot, but I never thought I'd owe you for saving my life."

"I was glad to do anything I could," she said softly. She regarded him for a moment, her eyes thoughtful. "What do you mean by saying you owe me a lot?"

He closed his eyes and made no answer, for he could not tell her now. Thinking he had dropped off to sleep, she did not press the question, and it was moments later before he asked: "Was it Quinn who got me?"

"No, Quinn was on his way home from Trout Creek when it happened. It was a man named Shafter. Highpockets said he was the one who brought the note."

"One of Bull's freighters."

"Yes, and it was probably Bull who fixed up the murder trap. Shafter was waiting outside to get you if Franz missed. They're both dead."

"Deborah was the one who wanted me killed," he said slowly.

"No, Lee," Hanna said quickly. "She had nothing to do with that note. She was playing cards with some friends of hers. It was a regular date she had once a week, so whoever planned to kill you knew she'd be gone all afternoon."

He let that thought lie in his mind for a time, feeling the relief it brought him and yet not fully believing it. He asked: "How long will I have to lie here?"

"Most of the month, I think."

He swore fiercely, and then, ashamed, he said — "I'm sorry, Hanna." — and, wearied, he dropped off to sleep again.

When he woke, Hanna was still there. "Highpockets said Jepson was trying to get you to sell to Quinn," he said.

"I haven't sold," she said quickly. "I made you a promise."

Relief washed across his face, and then pride, and Hanna smiled as she stood up and folded her sewing. "I told you, the first time you and Quinn argued with me, that I favored the Oregon Trunk. I still do."

He saw that she was troubled. She moved to the window, and stood looking out, the afternoon sun falling across her face and making her hair brightly alive. Lee, watching her, sensed the human warmth that was so much a part of her, the faithfulness, the gallantry, and a quick warmth rose in him.

Hanna turned from the window and came to the bed, worry still in her. "I don't know why Cyrus went over to the Harriman line. It isn't like him, because all the time I've known him, he's favored the people's railroad, and I see no reason for him to change. He says it won't pass, but, whether it does or not, I don't see that it makes any reason to go over to Harriman." She shook her head. "I don't believe in a lot of the things Jim Hill has done, but he is the one who broke the Harriman Fence. Lee, sometimes I wake up at night wondering if we'll ever get a railroad."

"You'll see steel before the end of the year," Lee said, "and you can help get it to Bend."

She regarded him soberly. "There's that old saying about a bird in the hand being worth two in the bush. When you feel like making out the forms, I'll sign. You can have your right of way, Lee."

He reached for her hand. "Soon as I see Highpockets, I'll have him get the forms and the checkbook." She was smiling down at him. Now, that the decision had been made, it seemed that a weight had been rolled away from her. There was a sweetness about her, a light and lovely quality he had never seen in her before. "I guess thanks just isn't a big enough word," he said.

"You don't have to thank me, Lee. Just see that the railroad is built. If there are any thanks to be given, I guess I should give them to you, because you haven't hurried me or started legal proceedings. Maybe I'm kind of silly that way, but I don't like being forced."

Her hand was still in his, vibrant and vital and alive. Without thought and with great urgency, he asked: "Will you marry me, Hanna?"

It was almost as if he had struck her. She drew her hand away and stepped back, her face utterly sober. "You don't have to repay me that way, Lee," she said gravely. "I wouldn't marry a man who asked me upon impulse because he thought he owed me something. Or when another woman is in his heart. I'm not big enough to share the man I love." Hanna whirled, and walked quickly out of the room.

He called — "Hanna, it wasn't that way!" — but she did not turn back. Presently he saw her walk past his window, heard the *crunch* of snow under her feet. He stared at the ceiling a long time. For the first time in his life, he had asked a woman to marry him, and she had said no.

There was a hurt pride in Lee Dawes, and then that passed, and he felt the deeper hurt. The full knowledge of how much he loved Hanna Racine came to him. It was not the feverish madness that had been in him when he had first seen Deborah on the *Inland Belle.* It was something else, something that had grown with the months and would continue to grow with the years, a comfortable love that made him miss her presence as he would miss a light taken from a room, leaving it in darkness.

Highpockets went to Madras for the right-of-way forms. Lee made them out, wrote Hanna a check, and Highpockets took them to her place. She had gone home the day he had asked her to marry him. Lee, hating the loneliness and the bed and the idleness, wondered about Hanna, and could not understand why she had left.

The signed right-of-way agreement was mailed to John Stevens, and a few days later Johnson Porter, on one of his quick trips through the country, stopped to visit Lee.

"Stevens doesn't know about the right of way yet, but he'll be tickled when he does," Porter said. "He's in Washington working on the Ellis Bill, which will give us the right to bridge the Columbia and Celilo Canal." He grinned. "The Union Pacific may kick up some trouble for us, but I wouldn't be surprised if we got around it with a little horse trading." Porter sobered. "Have you heard about the Smith homestead?"

"I just know it's down the river about Mile Seventy-Five."

Porter nodded. "A little above where we cross over to the east side. I told you they might come up with a high trump we didn't expect, and this is it. We thought we had that right of way sewed up, and our maps were approved at Washington before Smith got title to his homestead, but the point is he had filed while the approval of our maps was pending." Porter threw up his hands. "So there we sit, and we won't be able to do any grading through the Smith place till it's settled. He had prior rights, and he's commuted his homestead and sold to the Deschutes Railway Company."

"Then we'll relocate on the west side?"

"Not this late we won't. We've got the upper hand at the Crooked River crossing, especially now since you've got the Racine right of way. How did you finally manage it?"

"I guess Jepson did it for us when he started arguing with her about selling to Quinn." Lee reached for tobacco and pipe. "Say, can't you find anything for Highpockets to do? He just sits around keeping the seat of his pants warm."

"That's what he's supposed to do, along with keeping an eye on you. What if Boston Bull walked in and tried to finish the job they started in Madras?"

"I guess maybe he'd get it finished."

"That's right," Porter agreed. "As long as

you're on your back, Highpockets's job is to keep you alive."

"I'd like to stay alive long enough to finish the other half of the job Stevens gave me," Lee said.

"I aim to see that you do. I took this Jepson fellow rather lightly until the Madras business, but I don't now. I'd like to know why he changed sides and began talking Harriman to the Racine girl. That doesn't make any sense to me." Porter rose. "The doc says you'll be able to ride before long. When you can, you and Magoon are going to Burns. Stop at Jepson City, and talk to Jepson if he's there."

"Maybe I'd better shoot him," Lee growled. "I don't take much to the idea of being a clay pigeon for his trigger boys."

"I don't blame you, but don't kick up a ruckus unless you have to. Sometimes, just in talking to a man, you'll turn up something you don't expect. Go on over to the Malheur River. There are some survey crews working along it for Bill Hanley and Colonel C.E.S. Wood. If we build a line from here to Vale, it'll go down the Malheur, and it's possible Jepson may be playing an ace or two over there. Find out if they're having any trouble." Porter laid an envelope on the stand beside the bed. "This trip will take you three weeks. Maybe more. Stevens wants to know some things about the country that he didn't have time to get last summer. Mail the information to him in Portland as soon as you get it."

Highpockets came in after Porter left and sat down, long legs folded at the side of his chair, knees coming up almost to his head. He grinned when Lee said: "So you've been playing bodyguard."

"You're an important man," Highpockets said. "You know, I've been kicking myself for sending you into that, but Deborah . . . I mean. . . ." Highpockets floundered helplessly and stopped.

"Get it off your chest."

"She saw me coming into town that day after I'd delivered those horses. She stopped me, said she had to see you, but she allowed you wouldn't talk to her. Said she was in trouble with Quinn, and you could get her out. That's why I figgered the note was on the level."

"Maybe she did write it," Lee said somberly.

Highpockets shook his head. "Nope. Don't think so. But Jepson probably knew she wanted to see you, and he'd know when she played cards."

A week of warm weather in early February softened the snow to slush and took it off a little each day. Lee and Highpockets left town the last of that week, riding east through the junipers and past Millican's place beyond Horse Ridge, and came to Jepson City after dark.

"Fool notion," Highpockets growled. "They'll gut-shoot us before we get into the store."

"They won't know who we are till we get inside," Lee said, and swung down in front of the store.

Lee stepped into the building, one hand in his pocket, eyes raking the gloom of the store's interior. Jepson was not in sight. There was one man behind the counter, bald and bulging with fat, his long, yellow eyes glowering sullenly at Lee, who had come to a stop inside the door. The fat man began slowly to drift along the counter. "Stand pat, fatty!" Lee called. "Where's Jepson?"

"Ain't here."

"Where is he?"

"Bend."

"You're lying." Lee studied the fat man

intently, saw the yellow eyes flick toward the rear of the store and come again to Lee. "Watch him, Highpockets. I'm going to find Jepson."

Lee stepped into the storeroom, and closed the door into the front of the building. It was entirely black here, but on beyond a rectangular outline of light showed the location of a second door. Lee caught the animal smell of lard and bacon, the sharper odor of coal oil, the spicy scent of recently ground coffee, but through it all ran the stink of Cyrus Jepson's cigar.

Moving along an open aisle to Jepson's room, Lee put a hand on the knob, turned it quickly, and shoved. Jepson was at the desk, the cigar in his mouth a frayed stub, and, if he was surprised at Lee's appearance, he kept it from showing on his high-boned, red-cheeked face. He said: "How are you, Dawes? Come in."

"Surprised?"

"I learned some months ago not to be surprised at anything you do."

"I have a right of way through the Racine place."

"I know." Jepson tossed his cigar butt into a spittoon. "You've changed Hanna, Dawes, and it's too bad. She used to be a fine girl."

"You mean she was a girl who listened to

your advice. She hasn't changed. It was just too thick for her to swallow when you jumped to the Harriman people. What made you do that, Jepson?"

The little man fingered a new cigar he had taken from the box in front of him. "You wouldn't believe a lie, Dawes, and I'm not fool enough to tell the truth."

There was, Lee noted, a strained quality about Jepson's face, a quick, nervous movement of the fingers holding the cigar. Lee prodded: "Things been going your way, Jepson?"

"No, and the credit is largely yours." Jepson shrugged. "But the game is not lost and the stakes are still high. You'll remember we talked in Biggs about the cosmic principle of conflict, Dawes. You and I illustrate perfectly that principle." He smiled, apparently without guile. "We will continue to illustrate it until one of us is dead."

"Then let's stop illustrating. You have a gun, haven't you?"

Jepson built a steeple of his slender fingers, elbows on the desk, the smile still fixed on his lips. "I don't play that way, Dawes. I know people. I know that before we're finished, you'll walk into our guns. It would be very simple for you to kill me now, but you won't. On the other hand, I know the sort of bait a man like you can't turn down. When the time is right, I'll use that bait."

Lee, standing there at the door, his eyes locked with Jepson's round ones, felt the futility of this talk. Without a word, he stepped out of Jepson's office, pulled the door shut, and walked rapidly back to the front of the building. "Let's move," he said, and went on out.

Highpockets followed, eyes watchfully on the fat man until he had cleared the door. He ran to his horse, mounted, and cracked steel to him. It was not until the lights of Jepson's store had faded behind them that Highpockets took a good breath. He asked: "Learn anything?"

"Not much, except that Jepson is still a smart-talking *hombre*."

"You knew that," Highpockets said gloomily. "I still say it was a fool notion."

The trip along the Malheur took six weeks instead of the three Lee had expected, and, although he obtained the information Stevens wanted, he returned to Madras with the feeling that the time had been largely wasted. He had learned nothing more about Jepson's activities, and the driving compulsion to get this job done grew in him by the hour.

With his pipe loaded and drawing, Lee cruised along the street until it was dark, the cold March wind lifting dust and driving it with ceaseless, irritating energy. There was nothing here to hold him except an unfinished job, and discontent grew in him when he thought that Jepson might never make a fatal mistake or at least might not be prodded into it until steel reached Bend, and that was more than a year ahead.

Thinking of Hanna, Lee considered how different the world would be at this moment if she had said yes when he had asked her to marry him. He thought about the time she had told him life to him was a matter of rushing madly from one room to another, that he would never change, that he needed a room of his own. He would have made that room here in central Oregon if she had been willing to share it with him, but she had not, and her refusal laid a blight upon the future.

Lee swung back into the wind and returned to the hotel and to his room. The door was unlocked. He paused in the hall, wondering at this, right hand dipping into coat pocket for his gun. He drew it, and pushed the door open.

Deborah Quinn was standing by the window. She turned, smiling, and said gently: "Shut the door. I remember a few times when you came into my room without being invited. I'm returning the favor."

Chapter Eighteen

There was the same dark allure about Deborah's face there had always been, the exotic beauty, the red, full-lipped mouth, but as she came toward Lee, he saw that the slim grace that had characterized her was gone, that she moved with the slow awkwardness of a pregnant woman who had come close to the fulfillment of her destiny.

"Will you close the door, Lee?"

He did not want her here, did not want to talk to her, but he did close the door. He asked stiffly: "What about Mike?"

"He won't like it, but I won't be here long. You've got to help me, Lee."

"How did you know I was in town?"

"I paid a man here in the hotel to get word to me as soon as you got in, Lee. I was afraid you wouldn't come to see me, so I came to see you. Will you help me?"

There was a humility about her that was unlike her. Worry lines had appeared around her eyes and across her forehead. It had been almost a year since Lee had made that trip on the *Inland Belle,* hectic months that had brought more change to Deborah than to him. Studying her now, Lee could see little resemblance to the shapely Deborah Haig who had carried herself with so much regal pride.

"I'm remembering a promise you made me," Lee said. "When I got back to Shaniko, I found a note making another promise, but you married Mike the day you were to meet me in the Moro Hotel."

"You have such a good memory, Lee," she murmured. "Perhaps you remember telling me you loved me."

He had not, and he was surprised that she had asked. He said: "No."

"Or perhaps you can remember asking me to marry you."

Again he was surprised. He had never thought of it. He had seen Deborah and himself as the same kind of people: smart and worldly, understanding that when their time together had passed, they would separate, travel their own ways, and forget. He said: "No, I never did."

There was a small smile on her red lips. "I thought about it after you had left Shaniko that morning. You see, you and Mike looked at me differently. After you left, I knew how it would be. I'm not sorry for that night. I had to have it to get you out of my mind and to know I loved Mike. I had to find you were as cheap and irresponsible as you took me to be."

There was a strange irony in this thing — Mike Quinn's wife asking him to save their marriage. He hated Quinn. Quinn hated him. Yet, looking now at Deborah, there was a shame in him. He had hurt her more than she had hurt him, but not once had he thought about it that way. He would kill a man who looked at Hanna as he had looked at Deborah. And that was the way Mike felt about Deborah. Mike was right and he was wrong, and he felt the guilt that the knowledge brought him.

"You put it hard," he said at last.

"I'm being honest, Lee. I don't know much about love. I've had very little of it in my life, and it came on me suddenly. That morning after you left me in Shaniko, I married Mike because I loved him. I want to keep him . . . and I know I'm about to lose him. That's why I need your help."

"All right," he said heavily, and motioned toward a chair. "What do you want me to do?"

She moved back to the window, slowly,

and lowered herself into the chair. "I want to make a deal, Lee. I can clear up some things you haven't been sure about. In return, I want you to see Mike as soon as you can. Tell him you're not the father of my child."

"Maybe I am."

"No. I was two months pregnant. It's Mike's baby, and he's got to believe it before it comes. I didn't tell him when we were married, and, when he found out, he jumped to the conclusion that it was yours. He thinks you wouldn't marry me, and I married him just to give my baby a name."

Lee nodded, knowing the jealousy of which Quinn was capable, his quickness to anger and the depth at which his fury ran. "I don't think Mike would believe me," he said.

"You've got to make him believe you, Lee. I want my baby and I want a home and I want Mike. I don't know how you can do it, but there must be a way."

There was agony in her, as much agony as there had been in Mike the night he had found Deborah in Lee's arms. And because there was in Lee the sense of guilt for having brought this thing upon them, he said: "I'll do what I can."

She relaxed against the back of her chair,

as if his words had released a tension in her. She said: "Then I'll deliver my part of the bargain. You knew that I was associated with Jepson before I married Mike." Lee nodded, and she went on: "I teamed up with Jepson because he was a schemer and we both wanted money. We weren't very particular how we got it."

Lee had filled his pipe, and, lighting it now, he watched her and held his silence.

"Jepson knew that a railroad was bound to come. A railroad meant suckers, and Jepson was very good at separating suckers from their money. The trouble was, we'd had a bad deal on California real estate, and we'd lost about all we had. He fixed that by staking out Jepson City, running off a bunch of fake advertising folders, and sending them all over the world. He sold a lot of Jepson City property, but none around here. I doubt if three people in central Oregon ever saw one of those folders."

"Highpockets saw one. An Australian on the stage showed one to him."

"I know. That Australian stopped at Redmond and showed the folder to Herb Racine. That's why Jepson killed Racine. You see, Jepson saw that the people's movement was a way to make our fortune, and that Racine was the key man in the movement, so Jepson buttered him up until he had him where he wanted him. He even fooled Hanna, and she's sharper than her father ever was. Racine agreed with Jepson that the proper route for the people's railroad was to swing east through Burns and Vale and Jepson City. That railroad would have meant a million dollars for us. But Racine was too honest. The minute he saw the folder, he swore he'd expose Jepson and see that the railroad missed Jepson City by fifty miles. They had a quarrel in Redmond, and that night, when Racine was coming home, Jepson shot him."

"Racine didn't talk to anyone about Jepson?"

"No. Jepson promised to return the money and quit advertising until he did have a city. Racine believed him. I'm not sure, but I think the Australian is buried in the desert somewhere. I do know he threatened to make trouble when he saw Jepson City, and he disappeared rather suddenly. After that, Jepson expected to use Hanna the way he had planned to use her father, and he had fixed up some political connections himself. That's the way it was when we heard about the Hill and Harriman lines coming up the cañon. Jepson had seen Stevens somewhere . . . Montana, I think . . . and he heard Stevens was in a Portland hotel, registered under the name of Sampson. We went to Portland, stayed at the same hotel, and kept an eye on him. That's how we spotted you. I fixed it so you could talk to me on the *Inland Belle,* and wiggled my hips once or twice so you'd keep coming. You did, but I never succeeded in prying anything of much value out of you. I already knew Mike well, but neither Jepson nor I dreamed things would work out the way they did."

"Neither did I," Lee murmured.

"Mike didn't know about my connection with Jepson. He doesn't know yet as much as I'm telling you. He put me on a salary, and I traveled with him part of the time, because I knew the country and could help him with some of the people he had to deal with. Actually I was passing on to Jepson everything I found out from you and Mike. What we wanted to know mostly was whether either line was building across the desert and whether they'd follow the known surveys.

"What Jepson hoped to accomplish was to get the two lines to fighting so much that the Oregon Trunk would quit or sell out, and, if that happened, he thought the Harriman line would slow up or stop building entirely. Then the people would start thinking about the state-owned railroad again. Every move he made, such as that dynamite scheme and the time they tried to ambush you and all the rest, was made to make you or the Harriman people think the other side was doing the dirty work. Those schemes might have succeeded if you hadn't held back."

"You knew about them?"

"Not until afterwards, but I couldn't have stopped him anyway. He said my job was to spy on the men and his was to make our plan go. I failed because I began to think more of Mike than I did of my job, and Jepson failed because he couldn't stampede you into making a fight. Now he's changed his tactics. He's given up the people's railroad, but the Harriman survey across the desert runs through his property, and he plans to move his town site to it. The Hill survey misses him by miles, so he wants to hold the Oregon Trunk back and help the Harriman line beat it into Bend. Then he believes the Harriman people will build across the desert and he'll still win."

"Was he really drunk in Shaniko that time?"

"He never gets drunk. He's built that idea up until people believe it, and he uses it as an alibi."

"What about the time they tried to kill me at your place?"

"I don't know anything about that, Lee," she said earnestly. "It was Jepson, but I didn't have any inkling of what he aimed to do until we found you in the snow. Jepson is in love with me, or so he says, and he's bitter because I married Mike. He knew when I played cards, and I think the killing was planned to fix the blame on Mike."

"But Mike wasn't. . . ."

"He's crazy jealous, Lee. You know that. If he wasn't, he'd believe me. He's made some threats around town about what he's going to do to you, and it might have been hard for him to prove an alibi, because he was alone between here and Trout Creek."

Lee leaned forward, empty pipe held in his hands. "Will you tell this in court?"

She shook her head. "It would make me lose Mike, and I've been into too much of it myself."

"I've been able, through luck and using my head a little, to keep Jepson from doing too much harm," Lee said slowly, "but as long as he's alive and free, he's dangerous. He's just cagey enough so that I've never been able to get the proof I need."

"I'll go to court if it will help you, Lee,"

she said then, "and if you can get Mike back for me."

"He doesn't know about Jepson?"

"Not much, and he doesn't believe what he has heard. He thinks Jepson is just a smart-talking, insignificant little man who is betting on a long chance with his town site."

The door swung open, slamming hard against the wall. Lee came to his feet and, turning, saw Mike Quinn in the doorway, his cheeks ruddied by both wind and anger, his gray eyes made ugly by a compelling bitterness. He stood in silence for a long minute, and there was no sound in the room but Deborah's labored breathing. Outside in the street a drunken man raised a shout, and the wind roared around the corners of the hotel and sent an empty can *banging* down the street.

Lee said: "Come in, Mike. We were just talking about you."

"I'll bet you were," Quinn said coldly, "and I don't need to come in. I can do what I came to do from here. I found you two together once before in this hotel in a little different position. Isn't it enough for me to marry the. . . ."

"Mike!" Lee shouted.

Quinn waved a big hand in derision. "Don't like to hear it, do you? You aren't man enough to stand up and take the blame for what you've done. I can marry her and raise the kid. . . ."

"Shut up and listen," Lee cut in, anger cording the muscles of his jaws.

"Listen, hell! You've got nothing to say I want to hear. Jepson told me about that night in Shaniko a week before we were married. If it happened once, it could have happened before, and it leaves me just one answer to make."

Quinn's hand came from his pocket, a gun clutched in white-knuckled fingers, and Lee, standing helplessly across the room from Quinn, saw violent hatred sweep across the wide, craggy face.

"No, Mike, no!" It was Deborah, and she came too quickly from her chair. She stumbled and fell and did not rise.

Mike Quinn shoved his gun back into his pocket and there was horror in his eyes, as if he had just realized what he had planned to do. Then he came to her and, dropping to his knees, lifted her head. Her face was distorted as a spasm of pain swept through her. Then it passed, and she whispered: "Get the doctor, Mike." She tried to smile, and a hand came up to touch his cheek. "It's your baby, Mike. If anything happens to me, don't ever doubt it."

After Deborah was in bed in another room, and the doctor and a woman were with her, Quinn came back to stand in the doorway of Lee's room. He stared at Lee in silence for a time, shoulders hunched forward in a characteristic menacing roll; his face was sullen, but the violence of his anger was spent. "We'd better get a long ways apart, Dawes, and stay that way," he said bitterly. "We've always wanted what the other fellow had, but I won't share my wife."

"Funny thing, Mike." Lee got up and began pacing restlessly around the room. "I don't want Deborah. I asked Hanna to marry me, and she turned me down. I always thought I could have any woman for the asking, but when I find one I want to marry, I can't have her."

"Hanna? Well, I'll be damned. Jepson said. . . ."

"You're a bigger fool than I think you are, Mike, if you believe anything Jepson tells you. Why do you think he told you what he did?"

"He's just an old woman, I guess. Wanted to shove gossip along."

Lee laughed shortly. "If you had any

brains at all, you'd know he's been trying to get us to tangle all the time. You've got the woman that half the men in the country would give an arm to have, but you aren't satisfied. She came here tonight to ask me to tell you that it's your baby she's having and not mine. You've been jealous so long you're letting it make a bigger fool of you than Nature intended, and you're breaking the heart of the only woman who ever did love your ugly mug. Damn it, Quinn, you are a fool."

Quinn sat down on the bed and rolled a smoke and nursed the doubt that had been in him so long.

Lee watched him a moment in silence, and then said testily: "You gave me some sanctimonious talk about me bringing out the devil in a woman and you having respect for Deborah. Maybe if you could think back about nine months, you might remember at least one occasion when that respect kind of slipped. You don't think this kid isn't yours, Mike. You just think you haven't got all of Deborah, and you're so damned thick-headed you can't tell when you have."

Quinn threw his cigarette stub out of the window and brought his eyes to Lee's face. He said huskily: "We've fought and cussed each other, Lee, but we've never lied to each other. You aren't lying to me now, are you?"

"I'm not lying, Mike," Lee said.

They waited through the long hours until, near dawn, a woman came to stand in the doorway, a small, blanket-wrapped bundle in her arms. She said: "Your wife thought you'd want to see him, Mister Quinn."

Quinn came to his feet, eyes briefly on Lee, and then he slowly crossed the room, and stood looking down at the baby. He remained there a long time, and Lee came to stand behind him. He laughed, a great belly laugh that broke the tension. "The spit'n image of you, Mike. Red hair, flat nose, and an ugly Irish mug if I ever saw one."

"Ten pounder," the woman said, and took the baby away.

Pride was in Mike Quinn then. He stood with his shoulders back, doubt drained fully out of him. "He's a fine broth of a lad, and that's a fact. We'll call him Michael O'Brien Quinn."

"That's a hell of a thing," Lee jeered. "Whoever heard of O'Brien for a middle name?"

"I can't think of any name that's more Irish than O'Brien," Quinn said stiffly.

They faced each other, and it was as if a great tide had washed the rancor from them. Slowly Quinn held out his hand, and Lee took it.

"I'm sorry, Lee," Quinn said huskily. "I'm going to ask her to forgive me."

"She'll forgive you, Mike, because she loves you. I've been thinking some about what I'll be doing when this railroad gets finished. There'll be a lot of building here in central Oregon. Maybe we could team up in a construction business. We could have a sign that said 'Quinn and Dawes. We build anything.' How does that strike you?"

A grin lighted Mike Quinn's craggy face. "That'd be fine, Lee. It sure would."

CHAPTER NINETEEN

Construction was at its height this spring of 1910. Strung the length of the cañon, nine thousand men pounded and dug and blasted. With shovels and pickaxes, drills and dynamite, they inched their way along the rock walls, clawing out a forty-foot shelf until there was a hundred miles of grade — and first steel was laid at the mouth of the Deschutes. Ahead of them the engineers hung from ropes along the sheer walls of the cliffs and charted the plans for those behind.

While man with his weapons of violence altered swiftly the face Nature had given this earth, the river kept steadily on, growling and slowly gnawing a deeper channel, as it had for unmeasured time. And atop the west rim, Indians on the Warm Springs Reservation pondered the strangeness of this white race that had waited so long, and then in a sudden burst of wild energy had started pushing two paths of twin steel up the cañon.

Dozens of human difficulties must be worked out. They ranged from the job John F. Stevens had helped to do in Washington in getting the Ellis Bill passed, authorizing the Oregon Trunk to bridge the Columbia at Celilo, to agreeing upon the depot site in Madras. But toughest of all for the Oregon Trunk was the high trump the Harriman interest had played — the securing of the Smith homestead at Mile Seventy-Five that set athwart the Oregon Trunk right of way in the cañon, exactly as the Girt place had set athwart the access road to Horseshoe Bend.

Both sides recognized the Smith place as the strategic key to the battle. Oregon Trunk construction was held up at this point for two months. George W. Boschke, chief engineer of the Harriman Northwestern System, and builder of the Galveston sea wall, was in camp when a messenger rode in on a lathered horse and handed him a telegram that said that the Galveston sea wall had been carried away by another great hurricane. Boschke read it, and smiled. He said: "This telegram is a lie. I built that wall to stand. Double the force on Mile Seventy-Five." Boschke was right. The message was based on a false report, and the Harriman people hung doggedly to their obstructing position.

March spun out with its driving wind that pierced a man's clothes and flesh and laid its sharp chill into his bones, then April, with its clear skies and days that were longer and warmer and full of spring's eternal promise. The bunchgrass began to grow, and a slow green came to the valley floors. Meadowlarks sang lustily, and their melody, drifting with the wind and coming to Lee Dawes's ears, sent his thoughts trailing back over the months. Centering those thoughts was the image of slight, pretty Hanna Racine, who had said she would not marry him.

Lee was standing in front of the Green Hotel in Madras on the May morning that Highpockets braked a new automobile to a stop and called with great pride: "What do you think of this here contraption, son?"

"The contraption's all right, but you sure look out of place sitting behind the wheel. Don't you feel kind of funny without a fistful of ribbons?"

Highpockets climbed out and shook down the linen duster that he was wearing. "The way I figger it, the horse is done. We ain't gonna have no more use for 'em. Folks are gonna travel in these dad-burned gas buggies, and I'm never one to stand in the road of progress. So I up and bought me a car. Let's go for a ride. Ain't got nothing to do, have you?"

"Not right now. Just got back from Grizzly Butte. Some of the freighters forgot they had a contract and started hollering about not getting enough for hauling lumber."

"Jepson?"

Lee shrugged. "I figured it was, but no sign of him or Bull."

"Any trouble?"

"Not after I busted a couple of noses. Busting noses always goes a long way toward ending trouble if you bust the right noses."

"I knew I shouldn't have gone to Portland," Highpockets said sourly. "Might have knowed I'd miss some fun. Climb in. Let's go."

Lee didn't think to ask where they were going until Highpockets turned off the road at Hanna's place. "What the hell, you strung-out wash line," he said irritably. "She don't want to see me."

"You're an ignorant cuss for a feller who allows he knows all about women. Now shut up."

They bounced over the twin ruts and turned into the ranch yard, Highpockets pulling on the steering wheel and yelling: "Whoa!" Then he thought of the brake and looked at Lee a little sheepishly. "Sometimes I forget what I'm driving. Kind of scares me when I think I've got forty-eight horses out there in front."

Lee stepped down and knocked on the front door, but only the Indian girl Mary was at home.

"Miss Hanna out riding," Mary said. "You wait. She soon be back."

It was half an hour before Hanna rode in. She waved when she was still in the junipers and some distance from the house. When she rode around the barn, and reined up, Willie circling her mount and yapping ecstatically, she called: "It's nice to see you two, but I don't think there's a thing in the house to eat, Highpockets!"

Willie came bounding across the barnyard, and Lee, catching the dog, turned him over on his back, and roughed him up for a moment until Willie broke loose and went tearing back to Hanna.

She said: "I guess he'll never forget a favor, Lee."

"Memory like an elephant," Lee said, and thought of the frigid welcome he'd received when he'd brought Willie. He had spent a bad thirty minutes wondering how she would treat him, but when she stepped down from the saddle, a pleasant, smiling girl who was genuinely pleased to see him, he saw that he had worried needlessly.

"I was beginning to think you'd left the country, Lee," Hanna said, "after you'd got your right of way."

"I wanted more than that," he said more sharply than he intended. "I was after the top prize, but I didn't get it."

"Oh." There was the whisper of a quick breath, and the color of her cheeks deepened.

"I want to show off my new auto," Highpockets cut in. "Figgered you'd like to take a ride."

"I'd love to. It's a beauty, Highpockets."

"I'm right proud of her." The tall man glowed. "Dad-burned near as proud as I was of that black gelding I bought off you . . . the one that ran away from all them other horses in the races at Prineville."

"They're firing some coyote holes on Willow Creek," Lee said. "Let's go watch."

"Wait till I put on a dress." Hanna motioned to her Levi's. "These won't do in Madras."

Lee watched her run into the house, a straight, lithe figure, and he wondered at the hunger for her that rose in him. He tried to think ahead, to think around this girl who said she would not marry a man who asked her upon impulse or who held another woman in his heart, but he could not. His job with the Oregon Trunk would soon be ended, and the trail ahead seemed somber and without interest.

When they reached the site of the blast and saw the crowd, Hanna said: "Looks as if most of Madras is here."

"It'll be a good show," Lee said. "They've got six hundred kegs of powder in that cliff."

It was a good show; a great mass of earth and rock was hoisted into the air more than a hundred feet, hung there an instant as if defying the law of gravity, and then came crashing down on the opposite side of the cañon, the earth shaking with the impact of it as dust rose and swirled skyward. Rocks avalanched down the side, and their going brought others. It was minutes before the rumbling and shifting ceased, leaving the new face of the cliff brightly raw.

As they turned back to the car, Hanna asked: "Is it true that the Harriman people are quitting?"

"Just a rumor," Lee answered. "They are all denying it."

Highpockets snorted. "They ain't gonna quit as long as they're holding down the

Smith place like they are."

"Jim Hill's been in Portland," Hanna said suggestively. "Perhaps they've done some trading."

"I've been having the same idea," Lee said. "Nobody can build railroad the way things are now, and that doesn't suit men like Hill and Stevens. There's another rumor about the Oregon Trunk canceling the work south of Bend."

They had reached the car, and Hanna turned now, troubled eyes on Lee. "Does that mean they won't build across the desert?"

"I don't know, but there will be a railroad into Bend. How did you hear that rumor about the Harriman line?"

"Jepson told me. He's worried about the future of Jepson City, and he's still terribly angry because I sold you the right of way."

"Jepson is a different man from the one you had him pegged for," Lee said gravely. "He's a scheming devil who's used his friends to make a fortune out of Jepson City. He's done the same thing with the people's movement, talked big and fine about ideals that didn't mean a thing to him."

"I know," Hanna said slowly, and stepped into the car.

They said little on the way back to the Racine place, Hanna staring at the snow-peaked Cascades, which were alive now with the sunset's transient glory. Lee, glancing often at her, wondered if she suspected who had killed her father.

It was dusk when they stopped before Hanna's house, a lighted lamp in the front room signaling a welcome to them. High-pockets heaved a long sigh. "Sure is tough having to wait this long for supper."

"Empty all the way down through your hollow leg, I reckon," Lee said.

"Sure am. Hanna, I'm hoping that there Mary girl has enough supper fixed to keep me from starving complete." Highpockets got down and stamped into the house.

"Jepson has tried to stop us," Lee said, "using his own methods. And he's been slick enough not to leave much of a trail. I think he'll do something a little more direct before he's licked, and, when he does, I hope you will forgive me for what I have to do."

"There will be nothing to forgive," she said. "I found out what he was when he tried to get me to sell to Quinn."

Hanna started to step down, and Lee put a hand up to help her. Then, for apparently no reason at all, she slipped and fell and Lee caught her. She lay in his arms, her face a blur in the twilight, her eyes on him, and she was soft to his touch. He let the wildness in him go and, bringing her to him, kissed her in a hard, hungry way. She clung to him, her arms tightly around his neck, and there was that about her that carried him far out into a deep, uncharted sea.

He let her go and stepped back. "I'm sorry. I suppose now you'll like me less."

She made a still, vague figure against the car. "Why?"

"When I asked you to marry me, you said you'd never marry a man who asked you on impulse. It wasn't impulse, Hanna, and there is no other woman in my heart."

"You had been close to death," she whispered, "and I was there beside you. I'd let you have the right of way. You felt an obligation." She paused, and then added: "Quinn had married Deborah not very long before."

"I had never asked Deborah to be my wife," he said quickly. "I'm asking you again, and I won't believe you if you say no, after the way you kissed me."

Still she did not move or speak, and the minutes ran on into what seemed an endless silence. There was something else that had to be said, and her answer waited for it. He said: "There'll never be another woman like you. I shouldn't say what I'm saying, but it's the way I feel, and I've got to say it. I love you."

She gave her lips to him again, and, when she drew away, she said: "You remember that time in Bend when you told me that someday I'd forget myself? You've made me do that, Lee."

"I haven't heard your answer to my question."

"Yes."

"Tomorrow?"

She laughed. "You're never one to wait, are you?"

"There's no sense in waiting, Hanna, for something you want, when there's no reason for waiting."

"All right, Lee," she said, her voice so soft that he barely heard. "Tomorrow."

Riding back to Madras that night with Highpockets, Lee Dawes smiled in the darkness as he thought about the way Hanna had fallen into his arms, and he wondered if she had tripped purposely. One thing he did know. There were capacities in Hanna Racine that he had never suspected.

CHAPTER TWENTY

When Lee returned from Hanna's place, Johnson Porter was waiting for him in the lobby of the Green Hotel. "Did you get that trouble at Grizzly Butte straightened out?"

Lee nodded. "No sign of Jepson or Bull, but it's the same kind of play they've been pulling off."

"You'll soon have some sign of them," the contractor said soberly. "I've got news, and I'm curious to see if you read it the way I do. We've come to an agreement with the Harriman people regarding the Smith ranch, so there's nothing to keep us from building into Bend at our own speed."

"Then Jepson either has to shoot or quit."

"That's the way I see it. Here's what we did. The Deschutes Railway gets running rights over the twelve miles on the east side where we had each other tied up. Besides that, they get free use of our bridge over Crooked River and running powers to a point five hundred feet south of Redmond. On the other hand, they will convey to us at cost a right of way through the Smith place, and grant permission for the overhead crossing at Celilo. They also let us have, for a consideration, the necessary right of way between the mouth of the Deschutes and Celilo."

Lee stared thoughtfully at Porter for a time. "That puts a new slant on things," he said. "If there's any building across the desert, I guess we'll do it."

"That's right." Porter looked at Lee sharply. "What are you driving at?"

"I can promise you one thing about Jepson," Lee answered. "He won't pack up his valise and move out. He's figured all the time he could make us tangle with the Harriman people, and this agreement won't change his mind. It may bring him into the open, but it won't stop him."

Porter rose. He pushed a palm of a hand across his long, sober face, and shook his head. "It's your job to stop him, Lee," he said, and left the hotel.

For a long time Lee sat beside the window in his room, smoking and thinking about what Porter had told him. From what he knew now he couldn't begin to anticipate Jepson's next move, but he was certain of one thing: the little man was possessed of an inordinate pride that would keep him from quitting as long as life was in him.

A sharp knock brought Lee out of his chair and across the room, one hand clutching gun butt. Opening the door, he saw that it was the night clerk.

"A feller just rode up, came in, and gave me this." The clerk handed a sealed envelope to Lee. "Laid a dollar on the desk and told me to give it to you *pronto*."

Lee took the envelope. He said — "Thanks." — and tossed the clerk another dollar.

The envelope contained a single sheet of paper. Written in the same fine hand that had brought Lee to the Quinn house that snowy December day were the words:

I told you that you were a sucker for the right bait, Dawes. We've got Quinn in the old Calder house. You think you're tough enough to get him out by yourself, and you'll walk into our guns just like I said you would.

Quickly Lee slid into his coat, shoved his gun into his waistband, and, stepping into the next room, woke Highpockets. The tall man yawned, and came completely awake when Lee said: "Get your gun, pard. We're winding it up tonight."

"I'll put on my pants first." Highpockets threw back the covers. "What's up?"

Lee told him about the note. Highpockets made no comment until he was dressed and reaching for his coat. Then, glancing obliquely at Lee, he said: "I ain't one to duck a fight, son, but I also ain't one to start looking for hot lead if it ain't plumb necessary. Now it looks to me like we'd be downright foolish to walk into their guns like Jepson says."

"Then we're foolish. Let's roll."

"You oughta let the sheriff know," Highpockets said doggedly.

"You think we'd better ride over to Prineville, get the sheriff out of bed, and have him tell us to go to hell because we woke him up. Come on."

Highpockets held his silence until they were in his car and headed north from Madras. Then he asked: "You reckon Jepson's really got Quinn?"

"He wouldn't have written that note if he didn't. He's full of tricks, but he don't bluff."

The car raced on through the sagebrush, the rimrock a black line against the dark sky, bright stars making their distant and ineffectual light. Highpockets cleared his throat. "We've been through a pile of fighting since that time you sided me in Shaniko, but I never went into a ruckus blind. What in the name of Goshen are we up to?"

"We're going to put an end to Jepson's cussedness."

"Stop the car in front of the Calder place, walk in, and get shot to ribbons? I ain't in favor of it, Lee."

"It won't work that way. Jepson's tricky and he knows we know it, so he'll expect us to take the long way around and try to out-trick him. We'll go at it the short way, and I think we'll fool him."

"Maybe you've even got it figured out why he made this play," Highpockets said sarcastically.

"I think I have. There's only one way he can figure. He knows that if a railroad goes across the desert, it'll be ours and not a Harriman line. He knows we won't even come close to Jepson City. So he doesn't have any choice but to go back to the people's railroad, which will go through his town."

"That's a dead pigeon."

"It goes on the ballot," Lee reminded him. "A lot of things could happen between now and fall that would start the voters thinking about it."

"Like what?"

"Suppose we don't build south of Bend. Or don't build across the desert. He can say we've only done half a job. You told me yourself he's built up his own political connections."

"That's right," Highpockets admitted, "but what's that got to do with getting you and Quinn out here?"

"We'll find out," Lee answered.

The Calder place lay close to the Deschutes Railway grade, a two-story farmhouse that had been deserted, since it stood beside a ridge that had been pierced by a deep cut because of the blasting. Lee had seen the house from the road, and had noticed how the windows had been shredded by flying rocks. He thought about it now, fixing every detail in his mind. He asked: "Have you been inside the Calder house?"

"Yep. Big living room across the front, kitchen behind it, and a couple of bedrooms off to the side. More bedrooms upstairs."

They came within sight of the house, the windows along the front making pinpoints of light. The rest of the house was dark. "Ain't it funny they'd have a light in the front room?" Highpockets asked.

"Damned funny. Can you drive in close, so I can hit the porch in one jump?"

"Sure. Ain't nothing to stop me. Now, are you aiming to tell me what we're gonna do?"

"You'll make a wide swing in front of the house, slow down like you figured on stopping, and then speed up. They'll think you got scared and decided to go on. I'll hit the porch in front of the second window. You stop after you get past the house. Stay in the car and keep your eyes open for anybody they've got hid out."

Highpockets groaned. "I don't want to miss the whole shebang."

"You won't. Jepson'll have a man or two in the yard, and, if you don't get 'em, they'll get me. Plugging me in the back would be as easy as shooting pigeons in a haymow."

"Risky business," Highpockets grumbled.

"Jepson told me in his store, that time, he knew the kind of bait I'd take. I wouldn't turn this down in a million years . . . the way he threw it at me."

"Dad-burned idiot."

"That light is the trap. They'll figure on me dodging the light and sneaking around to the back. That's where they'll be all set to burn me down. The last thing they'll expect me to do is to bust into that lighted room."

Highpockets sighed gustily. "Your dad-burned pride will make a corpse out of you, but I hope you're right, son. I hope you are."

They swung off the road toward the house, headlights throwing a weird bright-ness upon the sagebrush. Lee's gun was in his hand, the door held open, as Highpock-ets swung wide in front of the house and made a quick turn, the wheels almost touch-ing the edge of the porch. Lee jumped, crossed to the window in two strides, and glimpsed the fat, bald man he had seen in the Jepson City store. A single lamp was on a box in the center of the room, the light shining through a smoky chimney and leav-ing the corners of the room in murky dark-ness.

An open door on the far wall led, Lee guessed, into the kitchen. The fat man had called through it, and was turning just as Lee touched the porch. He saw Lee at the window, and lifted his gun and fired, the bullet breathing through the glassless win-dow. Lee shot him. As the fat man fell, Lee shoved a leg through the window. It was then he saw Mike Quinn, face down on the floor a few feet beyond the lamp.

Lee paused in the window, stunned for an instant into immobility. A fury rose in him, a fury that sent a red wave rushing across his brain and caused him to cry out involuntarily: "Quinn's dead."

A gun sounded from the blackness of the yard, the bullet splintering a board six inches from Lee's head. He heard Highpockets's answering shot. He came on into the room, eyes raking the shadows for movement and finding none.

Outside, the firing had stopped. A man's heavy, running steps sounded in the back of the house. Lee fired through the door into the kitchen. The rhythm of the steps was broken. Boston Bull stumbled into the room, carried by the impetus of his run, hands outstretched as if to catch himself. He fell headlong, a loose, heavy weight, the house shaking with the impact of his big body. His gun had dropped from his hand, and he had come on past it. Now he saw the fat man's gun, and picked it up. Still lying flat, he whipped the revolver into position, and dropped it as Lee's second shot took life from him.

These fast-paced seconds had caught Jepson's men off guard because Lee had not reacted to plan. Two were dead, and Lee could reasonably assume that Highpockets had taken care of a third outside. But Jepson was still alive.

Lee shot out the light, knowing that the

advantage surprise had given him was gone now. The blackness was intense. For a time there was no sound. The smell of powder smoke was sharply pungent. Lee remained still, letting the long minutes pull out one behind the other. Jepson would break sooner or later. He'd know by now that Bull was dead, and panic would begin to have its way with him.

Then it came, the faint *creak* of a floor board, and mingled with the slowly receding smell of powder smoke was the foul reek of Jepson s cigar.

"You alive, Dawes?" Jepson called.

Lee made no answer. Jepson had not come into the front room. He was a man, Lee thought, of no great physical courage, but he had reached a point from which there could be no retreat. Now, having reached this place, he would be possessed by the kind of last-ditch daring that comes to a man when he has no choice but to go on.

"You're smart, Dawes!" Jepson called. "You didn't tackle this job like we thought you would."

The little man's voice was drawn wire-thin. He was silent again, and time ran on. Lee, shoulders pressed against the wall, could hear no sound but his own breathing.

"Damn you, Dawes!" Jepson screamed.

"Where are you?"

It was time now, Lee thought. He answered: "Waiting for you to come in, Jepson."

Lee stepped swiftly away from his position along the wall. As he moved, Jepson began shooting, raking the room with a wild, reckless fire. Lee dropped flat, lank body pressed against the floor. A bullet sliced through his coat, opening a bloody gash along his back. There had been six shots spread the length of the room. Lee came to his feet, and went flat again, for Jepson had another gun. He was firing more wildly than before, as if panic were pulling his trigger finger, one shot coming hard upon the heels of the one before.

Jepson had placed his shots at about the spot where Lee had stood when he had spoken. Lee circled quickly now, holding to the inside wall, and, when he thought Jepson had fired the last shell, he drove through the doorway, his own gun speaking.

It was the cigar that gave Jepson's position away, the glow of it a small red dot in the kitchen's blackness. Lee's first shot missed, the second fetched a long-drawn, gurgling sigh from Jepson. Lee held his fire then, sliding away from the door, and there was silence when Jepson's labored breathing stopped.

Presently, after the minutes had told Lee the danger was gone, he lighted a match. In the small flare he saw Jepson's high-boned face, round eyes staring upward in death's blankness. And he seemed to Lee in that moment to be a strangely inoffensive and futile little man.

Lee stumbled out of the house, breathing his lungs full of fresh air, feeling the release from the evil that had gripped this place. He called from the porch: "You all right, Highpockets?"

"Right as rain," the tall man answered. "You hurt?"

"A scratch along my back is all."

"Jepson?"

"Dead. I guess he'd smoked a cigar so long he forgot about having one in his mouth. Come here and give me a hand with Mike."

But Mike Quinn was not dead. He stared up at Lee in the light of the match Lee had struck, pale lips holding a small smile. "I came around in time to hear what you said," he whispered. "Funny Jepson going like that. Guess he wasn't so smart. He figured on making it look like you and me had plugged each other. Still thought he'd get the railroads to fighting. Reckon he died thinking it. Claimed he still believed in the people's railroad, but he was going to get you and me out of the way first. Said nothing he planned would work as long as you were alive. You had him worried, Lee."

Lee was on his knees beside Quinn, relief rushing through him, muscles weak with released tension. "How bad you hit, fella?"

"Not bad enough to die. I'm not going to die till I see that sign on Wall Street in Bend that says 'Dawes and Quinn, General Contractors.' I've got to live that long for Michael O'Brien."

Highpockets had found a lamp and lighted it. Lee, searching quickly, found a bullet hole high in Quinn's chest, another in his left shoulder. He asked: "What were you doing out here?"

"Coming after you." The small grin was on Quinn's lips again. "Got a message you were in trouble, but, hell, I should have stayed in town. You aren't worth coming out here after."

"Crank up your car, Highpockets!" Lee called. "I'll get this ornery, no-good pardner of mine into your back seat. I'm afraid he's going to live."

Railroad Day in Bend. The Oregon Trunk had won. Its rails had reached Madras on

February 15, 1911, with the Deschutes Railway still fifteen miles away. The Oregon Trunk swept on south with Bend as its goal. In September, Carl Gray, President of the OTL, announced that an agreement had been signed with the Harriman road for joint trackage between Metolius and Bend. Each road was to pay half the cost of maintenance. Joint terminals and warehouses at Bend were provided for, and Gray added that there would be no more railroad building in central Oregon for some time.

Now on this day, October 5, 1911, the job was done. The *click* of wheels on rails, the *hiss* of steam, the *chug* of power spinning out into movement, the long scream of a locomotive's whistle as it shrilled across a wide land — all were proof that a dream long held in human hearts had been realized.

Mayor Coe had proclaimed the day a holiday. Two thousand people gathered along the track to stare at the notables on the platform: Mayor Coe, bearded Jim Hill, his son, Louis Hill, Bryanesque Bill Hanley from Harney County, and others.

Lee Dawes stood at the edge of the crowd, Hanna on one side of him, Mike Quinn and Deborah, with Michael O'Brien Quinn in her arms, on the other. Lee watched Bill

Hanley lay the depot cornerstone, watched Jim Hill drive the golden spike into position, but he had only half an eye for this scene. He was remembering the night more than two years ago when he had first seen Shaniko and the raw, primitive quality of its life. It had been the old West, a West that would vanish now, to be remembered only at old settlers' conventions or in the comfortable warmth of a living room on a winter night when a new and young generation prodded a grandparent's memory.

Jim Hill had returned to the platform, and now he started his speech.

"Ladies and gentlemen, we are here today to celebrate the event of a new trail in central Oregon. This country, the entire Northwest, owes something to those who came before. They owe a great deal to the pioneers who took their lives in their hands, both the man and the woman, because it would have been a lonesome place for a man if the woman had not been willing to come."

Lee grinned as Hanna looked up at him. He winked at her, and whispered: "He's sure telling the truth." He put his arm around her, and Quinn, seeing it, needled him in the ribs with an elbow.

"Behave," Quinn muttered. "You're listening to a great man."

But the events of these last two years crowded into Lee's mind and closed his ears to Hill's words. The people's railroad had been defeated in the election, but Hanna argued stubbornly that it had accomplished its purpose, that Bend would not be celebrating Railroad Day if the proposal had not stirred Hill and Harriman into action. Lee argued as stubbornly that it was not true, that Hill and Harriman would have built, regardless of the people's line.

It was pleasant, this arguing with his wife Hanna, for he found capacities in her he had never dreamed a woman could have. It was the end of fury for Lee Dawes. There had been the wildness in him that had driven him from one job to another. That wildness would never be entirely gone — serenity and a day-by-day even tenor of living would never be for Lee Dawes — but there was a permanence, a direction to his life now, and it had been Hanna who had given it to him.

This was a bright land, a far-reaching land of junipers and pine and sage. There was a skyward tilt of the Cascades to westward, the high desert to the east, and there was a promise the land held for those who, like Lee and Mike Quinn, had come to exchange their work for the treasure it held.

Lee's arm tightened around Hanna. Again her eyes lifted to meet his, and for that moment Jim Hill and the two thousand people around them ceased to exist. It was a world for just two people in love. This was the way he wanted it. This was the way it would always be.

ABOUT THE AUTHOR

Wayne D. Overholser won three Spur Awards from the Western Writers of America and has a long list of fine Western titles to his credit. He was born in Pomeroy, Washington, and attended the University of Montana, University of Oregon, and the University of Southern California before becoming a public schoolteacher and principal in various Oregon communities. He began writing for Western pulp magazines in 1936 and within a couple of years was a regular contributor to Street & Smith's *Western Story Magazine* and Fiction House's *Lariat Story Magazine*. *Buckaroo's Code* (1947) was his first Western novel and remains one of his best. In the 1950s and 1960s, having retired from academic work to concentrate on writing, he would publish as many as four books a year under his own name or a pseudonym, most prominently as Joseph Wayne. *The Violent Land* (1954), *The*

Lone Deputy (1957), *The Bitter Night* (1961), and *Riders of the Sundowns* (1997) are among the finest of the Overholser titles. *The Sweet and Bitter Land* (1950), *Bunch Grass* (1955), and *Land of Promises* (1962) are among the best Joseph Wayne titles, and *Law Man* (1953) is a most rewarding novel under the Lee Leighton pseudonym. Overholser's Western novels, whatever the byline, are based on a solid knowledge of the history and customs of the nineteenth-century West, particularly when set in his two favorite Western states, Oregon and Colorado. Many of his novels are first-person narratives, a technique that tends to bring an added dimension of vividness to the frontier experiences of his narrators and frequently, as in *Cast a Long Shadow* (1957), the female characters one encounters are among the most memorable. He wrote his numerous novels with a consistent skill and an uncommon sensitivity to the depths of human character. Almost invariably, his stories weave a spell of their own with their scenes and images of social and economic forces often in conflict and the diverse ways of life and personalities that made the American Western frontier so unique a time and place in human history. *Beyond the Law* will be his next Five Star Western.